A Few Minutes Time

A Collection of Very Short Stories

Paperback Edition - ISBN 979-8-9880034-2-7

Published in the United States
by Stairns Media Publishing, Scottsdale, Arizona

www.Stairns Media Publishing

Introduction

Welcome to my compilation of Flash Fiction and Very Short Stories. A book where you can read a complete story without losing your place.

Authors spend years composing their grand manuscripts. But we don't always have the time and energy to sit down and immerse ourselves in A Tale of Two Cities or War and Peace.

During those periods between publishing an epic novel, most authors produce short stories. It helps keep their creative juices flowing. Just like a novel, a well-written short story can entertain and perhaps even help us reflect on who we are and what we do.

Whether you are reading this book in an airport, or a doctor's office, or you are just taking a short break from your daily grind, **A Few Minutes Time**, offers you a chance to escape from reality for a few precious minutes without the fear of commitment.

Some of the stories I have included here are pure fiction, straight out of my sometimes-convoluted mind. Other stories are memories from my past that you may find interesting. There may even be mention of a few places you recognize.

So, take a few short minutes to read one or two of my yarns.

I hope you enjoy reading them as much as I enjoyed writing them.

J. Salvatore Domino

I believe love can last forever. In this story, love abounds for our leading man, James, who refuses to let go of his wonderful lifetime of memories.

White Lace and Promises
An angel glimmering in white.

As the sun sparkled through the stained glass that ringed the top of the church walls, James surveyed the chapel room. He smiled, realizing all the people that he and Margie held dear, their friends and family, had filled the room.

He glanced down the aisle to see Margie in her white lace gown. To him, she was an angel. He could not help remembering how they met at the church social that summer afternoon. She was so young and innocent.

He could still see her long, dark hair cascading down over her shoulders. Her petite figure, accentuated by a pair of short, tight hotpants, caught his eye immediately. When she smiled, she drew him to her in an instant. He was smitten. Margie was not as interested, almost ambivalent to the attention of the tall lanky boy from across town. She didn't really care for the pencil-thin mustache he thought enriched his smile. His male friends seemed to like it more than the women. Even his mother commented that his whiskers made his nose look big. James didn't care what they thought, it was his style.

He worked hard to make Margie love him. Winning her over took longer than he expected. But back then, things were less complicated. Their first dates were simple pleasures. A stroll through the park, a meeting at the library, or sharing an ice cream cone on a hot summer day. They sat holding hands on a bench for hours, just talking.

Once, they went on a camping trip with a group of friends. They were both so slim they could fit into the same sleeping bag. Slender bodies being a treasure reserved for the young.

A kiss, in those days, was the limit of their affection. They would spend all day "making out" as they called it back then. There was no sex involved. They expressed their love through hugging and kissing.

Even then, James knew he was ready for a partnership. Margie was the one for him. Only a life together could bring them happiness. A future loaded with promises.

Oh, how he longed for those simple days again. But the changes had to come. Today would be the culmination of all they had worked for, together.

James looked ahead at the minister standing there so solemnly with his game face on. It was the same expression he wore regardless of the occasion. It could be the baptism of a newborn baby, the sacrament of confirmation, a wedding, or a funeral. They were all tasks that he had grown accustomed to performing for his disciples. When James nodded, the reverend read a brief prayer from the little black booklet in his hand.

James began to grow weak in the knees. Even when you know what is coming, it's difficult to imagine what lies ahead. But then the future is always uncertain. When he appeared to wobble, his best friend, Bart, who stood at his side, took his arm and helped him stiffen his posture. He wanted to look steadfast for his bride. She was there before him like an angel glimmering in white. It would be their last memory together.

As they closed the casket, he whispered goodbye to the love of his life. With the pallbearers in the lead, they walked down the aisle together one last time.

As an amateur tennis player, I compete against players from all walks of life. Wherever I go, I find camaraderie and teamwork.

But occasionally our competitive juices flow a little too strongly. The game, which is played for fun, becomes serious business.

In this story, two friends take the competition a little too seriously for their own good. The result is…

Assault With A Penn Four
Never apologize.

"You can't do that," Ansel shouted. "You nearly took my head off."

Greer flashed a wry smile across his face. "There is nothing illegal about it. Back up if you can't take it."

Ansel did not like being a target every time Greer had a chance to make a winning shot. In his mind, it wasn't good sportsmanship. He vowed revenge if Greer did not stop attacking him unnecessarily.

At the break for the court change, Greer grabbed his copy of The Rules of Tennis and thumbed quickly through the text. There was no mention of directing the ball in the direction of any player or any rules prohibiting it.

When they returned to the court, you could cut the tension with a knife. Once again Ansel took an aggressive position opposite Greer, hoping to make a quick point and secure the game.

Play continued at a normal pace until Ansel's partner Duncan returned a weak lob directly in line with Greer's forehand. Greer wasted no time in jumping on the weak shot and hammering a blistering shot right at Ansel's midsection. Ansel tried to avoid the rocketing yellow sphere but could not react fast enough. As he turned his body, he placed himself in a vulnerable position. The ball, traveling at over one hundred miles per hour, hit Ansel squarely in the gonads. He doubled over in pain, then fell, uncontrolled, to the hard surface of the court. He screamed in pain, "Ooow."

At first, Greer laughed. Much like watching home videos of someone falling off a chair. It was not until he realized he might truly have injured Ansel did he show any concern. "Hey, you alright?" he asked.

Ansel's face turned pale as he writhed in pain. With the wind knocked out of him, there was little he could do but lay there trying to recover. His partner, Duncan, tried to comfort him. "Just relax, take a deep breath," he said.

After a few minutes, Duncan helped Ansel to his feet and onto a nearby bench to regain his composure.

"That's it, Greer. You and I are through. I have had enough of your crap."

Greer shrugged, in an attempt to defend his action. "I was just trying to make a shot." Then, unsympathetically, he followed up with. "Next time get out of the way."

Ansel rose to his feet. It concerned the others that violence might erupt, but instead, Ansel grabbed his bag and angrily strode away off the court.

"You will be hearing from my lawyer," he shouted at Greer as he exited the tennis club.

Greer was unconcerned. No one ever called their lawyer over a tennis match. But that ended the competition for the day.

Greer's partner Wilton suggested he offer an olive branch. "You should probably call him to apologize."

"That's not going to happen," replied Greer. "He will cool down."

Two days later Greer was relaxing on his patio when his doorbell rang. He opened his door to find a courier. Before he could realize what was happening, the courier shoved an envelope into Greer's hand and declared. "You have been served."

Greer looked at the package in dismay. *What the hell is this?*

He tore open the seal on the envelope and pulled out an official-looking document. They intentionally left the first page blank, but on page two, the heading read:

IN THE CIRCUIT COURT FOR FAIRVIEW COUNTY,

"ANSEL TESTICLE et al" – Plaintiff

GREER SPHERE – Defendant

ONE COUNT of ASSAULT WITH PENN FOUR

The case became known facetiously as ***Ball vs. Balls***. Both of which were fuzzy and well-worn.

For some people, love can be a complex emotion. It may involve more than just two people. When it comes to love, sometimes we need to get our priorities in line.

The Tale of Rose Gray
<u>He made his choice.</u>

Brad and Tara were at odds. The last few days had been the most contentious of their time together. They glared angrily at each other. With tears streaming down Tara's face, she offered Brad an ultimatum. "It's time to make a choice. It's either me or your new mistress."

"Rose, her name is Rose Gray. Why can't you call her by her proper name?"

"Brad, I am tired of your crap. The two of you spend every waking moment together. You haven't taken me to dinner in a year. We have not made love in months. The other night I got dolled up in a sexy negligée and you didn't even notice. You came home and went straight to bed. You didn't even take your socks off."

"Quit being a drama queen, Tara. I was exhausted. I worked all day."

Tara stood fast. "What's it going to be? Me or your new love?"

"I am not giving up on Rosie," Brad insisted.

Tara wheeled around and strode off in disgust. As she climbed into her car, she exclaimed. "You will be hearing from my lawyer."

Brad pulled a chair up behind where Rosie waited patiently for him. He stroked her backside. "Don't worry, honey, nothing will come between us. From now on, it is just you and me, old girl."

True to her word, Tara filed for a divorce on the grounds of alienation of affection. Two months later, after a bitter negotiation period, they appeared in court.

The judge asked, "Are all parties present? Where is this Rose Gray mentioned in the testimony?"

Tara barked back. "No, Rosie is still back at our house, where he left her. He sleeps with her every night."

Brad added, "She can't come out right now."

The confused magistrate asked. "Why isn't she here at this hearing, and why can't she come out? What is her problem?"

Brad replied, "Her internals need to be reconstructed."

"What?" asked the judge.

"Rose is my 1963 Rose Pink Corvette convertible, with gray leather interior."

The judge rolled his eyes, then slammed down his gavel. "Divorce granted."

He awarded Tara the couple's entire estate. Minus Rose Gray, of course.

The older we get, the more memories we create. Many times, they are as clear as the day we lived them. Other memories we view through rose-colored glasses.

In this poignant story, one man's memories of life and love bubble up to the surface, reminding us of who we are and where we came from.

A Picture Worth A Thousand Memories
Fred could see into the past.

A wise man once said beauty is only skin deep. He, of course, meant physical beauty, as beauty takes on many forms. Beauty, or our perception of beauty, changes over time as we change over the years.

As a boy, I grew up with a large extended family. My parents, aunts, uncles, and cousins dined together, played together, and celebrated holidays as a group. Over time, we grew apart into a dozen smaller families.

My mom died at sixty years old of cancer, leaving my dad and me to grow old together. With the help of lots of friends and family, my father did well on his own. He never remarried, living to be seventy-eight before his health worsened and he passed away.

After the loss of my dad, I started growing closer to my uncle Fred. Fred, my father's younger brother, is an upbeat fellow who married my Aunt Chloe over fifty years ago. As a boy, I never thought much about Fred and Chloe. They were the aunt and uncle who came to visit us once in a while, or we would go visit them at their house.

One thing I do remember is that Aunt Chloe made the best Chicken Pot Pie on the planet. Young boys are often picky eaters, and I was one of them, but whenever Aunt Chloe brought Chicken Pot Pie to a family function, I ate heartily.

Now, once a month or so, my wife and I meet Fred and Chloe for happy hour at a local restaurant. It is our way of monitoring how they are doing in their advancing years. Every so often on my way home from work, I stop at the liquor store and buy a six-pack of an off-brand beer that Fred has been drinking since he was a young man. We share a couple of beers and Fred tells me stories of when he was young and how he and Chloe would travel across the country to see the natural wonders and rural parts of the country most people avoid.

A few weeks ago, I stopped by Fred's with my usual six-pack and found Fred in his office, staring at an old picture. It was a picture of my Aunt Chloe in her younger days. She looked beautiful in a pair of short pants and a crop top, her dark hair flowing softly across her shoulders. She had a captivating smile on her face. It was easy to see why Fred had fallen in love with her.

"I have always loved this picture. She is such a beautiful woman," he said.

It struck me that he said, "She IS a beautiful woman." Not, "She WAS a beautiful woman."

He went on to explain, "I took the picture in Holland, Michigan, at the annual tulip festival." They had gone there for a weekend getaway from their inner-city home in Chicago.

"We camped out in a tent, at a campground just outside of town. It rained all weekend. It was so muddy at the campsite that the floor of the tent was soaked. We had to sleep in the car. I remember it like it was yesterday. I keep this picture here in my office as a reminder of what a wonderful life I have had. Every day, I look at it and see the beauty that your aunt has been graced with." As he spoke, he put his glasses back on. It was as if the glasses were helping him to see into the past.

Fred and I sat out on his backyard patio while he relayed stories of his younger days. A few minutes later, Aunt Chloe brought a bowl full of corn chips out to us to accompany our beers. I had never noticed Chloe's beauty before. At seventy-two years old, she is now a petite, gray-haired woman who is more frail than robust. Yet when she smiled, I instantly recognized that same enchanting smile I had seen in the picture Fred showed me earlier.

She kissed Fred on the head as she warned him, "Don't drink too much. You won't sleep tonight."

Fred, acting the part of the tough old man, replied. "I am a big boy. I'll be fine." She left us alone with our beer and chips to chat. As soon as she went back inside, Fred beamed with pride, his happiness apparent.

That evening, I went home and found my wife reading a novel by J. Salvatore Domino, one of her favorite authors. I took her hand and looked deeply into her eyes. Becky will be fifty years old on her next birthday, but today I saw the same beautiful young woman I fell head over heels in love with nearly thirty years ago.

I held her in my arms and kissed her. She commented, "Someone's in a good mood."

I told her about my visit with Fred and asked her to do me a favor. I asked her to learn to cook Chloe's Chicken Pot Pie recipe. Already a good cook in her own right, my request surprised Becky. After I explained my penchant for Chloe's dish, she agreed.

I spent the rest of the evening digging through old photographs of Becky from our early days. I found a perfect picture of Becky at the wedding of an old friend. Her beauty and happiness were never more apparent. The next day I found a frame for the picture, and it now sits on a shelf in my office where I can see it every day.

A few days later, Becky invited Chloe and Fred to our house for dinner, understanding that the two women would make my favorite Chicken Pot Pie using Chloe's method. Fred and I watched the two women perform their magic on an eclectic mix of ingredients. The aroma was enchanting as it baked slowly in the oven.

The pie was everything I remembered. Even Becky expressed her admiration for Chloe's recipe. There was a certain satisfaction, a feeling of love that came with every bite. We ate as much as our stomachs would hold, then wrapped the leftovers for another meal. After Fred and Chloe returned home, Becky and I enjoyed a glass of our favorite white wine. Even though she had worked all day and all evening serving my whim, she was happy to take a few minutes to sit and talk.

That night, we made love like we were youngsters again. As I held her in my arms, appreciating the joy that came with a simple night of togetherness, she whispered, "Wow, what has gotten into you lately?"

"Darling, I have recently learned to appreciate all that I have and how much our life means to me."

In the last few weeks, my life has changed in more ways than I can count. We made a pledge to travel more. To make fresh memories and to take a lot more pictures of our journey through life. Every day I see my beautiful wife as both the woman she was and the woman she is. Every few weeks when she wants to surprise me, she makes my favorite meal and then takes my hand and carries me off to remind me why we have been together so long.

We still meet Fred and Chloe for happy hour and even though Fred's health is failing, he still maintains that ever-present smile whenever he looks at Chloe.

As for me, I have many good years ahead of me to enjoy my life, and for Becky's Chicken Pot Pie.

The world has shrunk as more and more of our lives happen in cyberspace. Relationships develop with others across the globe. Often, they are formed and discarded before we ever know what has transpired. Such was the case of My Quiet One.

My Quiet One
<u>We were almost there.</u>

Everyone called her, "The Quiet One", but to me, she was anything but quiet. The way her personality stood out above the others spoke loudly. Her smile screamed, "I am happy to meet you". The way her eyes sparkled, like diamonds against a black velvet cloth, intrigued me. Her playful expression made me want more.

The pure sense of delight I experienced at each encounter spoke for itself. I could not help but fall for her the moment I saw her.

I started slowly, not wanting to scare her away. Moving too fast would surely make me seem needy. Each day, like a peacock, I unfurled my feathers with witty sayings and tempting images. All the time praying, she would take notice. Hoping she would seek my friendship, my warmth, my devotion.

At first, I extended her a fleeting glance in passing. Hoping she might notice me. I simply wanted her to acknowledge my existence. Then I spoke up louder and in a more prominent voice. While I did not direct my comments to her, I made them in such a manner that she could not ignore me.

The strategy worked. Over time, she responded to my overtures. Soon we were exchanging ideas, offering opinions, and sharing the occasional laugh. We revealed our inner thoughts about life, love, and our future. She was no longer The Quiet One, and I could see deep into her soul. It was as if our love affair had been "pre-approved" by Cupid, no arrow necessary.

When she changed her hairstyle, she hadn't even left the salon before she asked me my thoughts on her new look. I remember the day she got a diamond-studded nose ring that contrasted with her ebony skin. She could not wait to see if I approved. With each change, she looked even more beautiful than when we first met.

I tried desperately to keep her attention. I bought new clothes that met with her approval. To look younger, I shaved my beard. When I showed her my new car, she begged me to take her for a ride. It took a long time but little by little I was winning her over.

Each time we chatted; my heart leaped with joy. Each night when we were apart, I wrestled in my sleep, anticipating tomorrow. A chance for us to meet again and resume our love affair.

We had come from different places only to meet in the here and now of our lives, as if destiny had called us to this place.

Then on a morning much like today, I made a mistake. I told her an off-color joke. I meant the comment to be funny. To her, it was insulting. In an instant, she changed. She grew cold, aloof, distant. Like her pseudonym, she became The Quiet One again.

Over and over, I looked for her, but she wasn't there. Gone like a ghost. Our love affair was lost in the cloud. A figment of my imagination.

Then came the notice. They had blocked our interaction. It was over, I would never *Tweet* my quiet one again.

For those of you who enjoy the outdoors, whether it be an easy stroll in the city park or a challenging trek up the side of Mount Kilimanjaro, you will enjoy this short adventure with our friend Jamie.

Jamie was enjoying a pleasant hike into the desert until this happened…

Hiking With Jamie
<u>A trail of an adventure.</u>

Jamie's eyes swept across the mountains that surrounded him. A blanket of wildflowers, bright yellow poppies, and deep purple lupine; carpeted the hillsides. The blooms, courtesy of abundant spring rains, made this hike into the desert foothills one of the things he enjoyed most about living in Arizona.

The solitude of hiking alone deep into the desert made him both joyful and nervous. He hadn't seen another human being on the trail for at least twenty minutes. He could do without the throng of winter visitors that crowded the trails this time of year. Yet the sign at the entry to the trailhead warned of encounters with post-hibernating wildlife. The absence of cell service meant he was alone, isolated from any help, should he need assistance.

As he stepped over the rise, the flora gave way to dry rocky terrain. A half-mile ahead, the trail narrowed, heading down toward a dry riverbed. The pathway wound between two boulders where a two-foot drop-off had developed. He would have to watch his step on the loose gravel at the base of the dry wash.

When he stepped down from the firm ground, he heard the familiar sound of a Diamondback Rattler. Looking down, Jamie found himself face to face with an ominous viper, all curled up and ready to strike. Before he could react, the six-foot demon sprang, narrowly missing Jamie's leg with its first attack. Jamie nearly lost his balance, scurrying back up to the solid ground of the trail and out of striking distance.

Jamie had seen the pictures of unsuspecting hikers, who were caught daydreaming. Their arm or leg swollen to a hideous size. The skin beginning to discolor as the poisonous venom spreads through the injured tissue. He heard the stories of how they fought against time to seek medical attention. Some made it, some didn't.

For now, he was safe. But he needed a plan of action. The rattler showed no signs of wanting to move out of his comfortable resting spot and Jamie had no way to encourage him to leave. He gazed around for a stick, a tree branch, anything he could use to shoo the menacing beast out of the way. The dry desert trailhead provided little natural resources he could use as a weapon.

His only recourse was to grab a handful of rocks and bombard the monster with stones. His first couple of attempts missed their mark. The dangerous reptile remained unfazed. When his third attempt seemed to hit the target, he thought he was home free. But the assault only angered the snake even more, hissing and rattling in an intimidating fashion.

It was time to decide, find another way around the problem, or retreat up the trail, a distance of several miles. He gazed up and down at the rocky terrain he would have to traverse to bypass the bottleneck, and it looked even more threatening than the dry riverbed. *Who knows what dangerous creatures are hiding under those rocks? Bobcat? Javelina? Scorpion? More Snakes?*

The snake had Jamie trapped. His only choice was to wait it out, hoping the snake will move on. As he paced back and forth on the groomed portion of the trail. Out of nowhere, a gray-haired gentleman, a seasoned and experienced hiker, appeared on the other side of the wash.

Dressed in little more than a T-shirt, shorts, hiking boots, and a beige "boonie" hat, he looked like easy prey for the treacherous viper.

Jamie cried, "Sir, watch out! There is a rattler right in front of you."

The cantankerous old guy glanced down at the snake, who sat coiled and ready to strike. He waved his hand in front of the creature, who immediately uncoiled half the length of its body. It positioned its fangs to bury themselves in his flesh. The old man shifted his hand just in time to avoid the predator's bite. Then, just as swiftly, he grabbed the demon by its rattle and with one continuous motion flung it high up the rocks, away from any harm.

The old man stepped up from the wash, looked at Jamie, and said, "You're welcome." Then he strode past Jamie and headed up the trail. In seconds, he was out of sight.

Jamie couldn't believe what he had just witnessed. Still awestruck, he whimpered, "Thank you."

Immigration, whether legal or illegal, is no joke. As people move about the globe, they become foreigners in a foreign land.

Benaim And The Wall
It was "Foreigner Go Home".

Emoni paced the floor, waiting for Ben to return. He was out on the golf course and his phone calls were being routed to voicemail. That wasn't unusual. His phone was likely in his golf bag. He didn't like being disturbed during a critical putt.

"How could this have happened?" she cried.

The U.S. closed the border and there wasn't any indication of when it would reopen. They interrupted the local television programming with news of Canadians fleeing the U.S. with only the clothes on their backs. News videos already showed Border Patrol troops erecting temporary fences to restrict travel until they can complete a new permanent wall. Videos showed people caught trying to cross the border being held in temporary containment vessels. Families were being separated; children were detained in cages like wild dogs.

Outside Em's Arizona home, a crowd gathered. In a matter of minutes, Jeeps and trucks of all types crowded the street. Men in militia uniforms with AR-15s milled around. Other less ominous-looking protesters carried signs, "Foreigner Go Home."

Ben had to fight his way through the burgeoning crowd to get into his garage.

"What the hell is going on, Em?"

"I don't know. It all happened so fast. I got a text from the airline. They have canceled all flights to Canada. I don't know how we will get home?"

Then came the pounding on the front door. Benaim peeked through the door's peephole. He saw two uniformed men holding up credentials from the U.S. Citizenship and Immigration Services, in plain sight of Ben's peephole view. Cautiously, Ben opened the door.

"Benaim Coulter? Marshall Kelly, Immigration. Records show you entered the U.S. from Ottawa, Canada, one hundred seventy-eight days ago. Sir, do you know Canadian citizens can only stay in the U.S. for a maximum of one hundred eighty days without an extension?"

"Yes, officer. We had planned to leave tomorrow. We just received word that the border is closed, and they canceled our flight. As soon as the border reopens, we will be on our way."

"Sir; the border may not open for months. You must leave before your deadline. No exceptions. I suggest you make other arrangements. If you are found here in two days, you will be arrested."

"What other arrangements can we make?" Ben asked.

"Get to the nearest border crossing. You have two days. I will do my best to disperse this crowd; I suggest you leave immediately before they get ugly."

Ben looked at Em. "What will we do?"

"We have to find another way to return home."

Driving from Arizona to the north border was out of the question. The distance was too great. Flying to a U.S. border city like Detroit or Seattle could not guarantee a safe border crossing in time.

Emoni searched the internet for options. There had to be some way. "Look," she declared. "The border to Mexico is still open."

She booked the last two seats on a flight from Tijuana, Mexico, to Ottawa for the next morning. They packed as much as they could carry into their suitcases and headed south to the border. In four hours, they would be safe in Mexico and headed for the true north.

All the way to the border, Ben and Em sang, **"O Canada! Our home and native land!"**

The following is a true story, somewhat embellished, but true.

How A Fat Man Turned Me Into A Criminal
I was duped by a small-time crook.

Here is a story I have kept under my hat for a very long time. Which in itself is a significant achievement, since I rarely wear a hat. I thought it would be okay, at this late date in my life, to spill my guts because the players in this story are mostly dead. That is, I mean, most of them are dead, not mostly dead, like Westley in The Princess Bride. They are all the way dead, at least most of them.

The tale is about a fellow I used to call "The Fat Man". I don't remember his real name; it was something like Mark or Marty, but myself and my friends always referred to him as The Fat Man.

The Fat Man, as you might guess, was a large man, well over six feet tall and grossly overweight. An imposing figure with dark hair, displaying only a few wisps of gray and a full beard that had more gray hairs than his head. He appeared, at the time I knew him, to be in his early to mid-forties. The Fat Man was a tough-looking guy who had survived a few tours in Joliet Penitentiary outside Chicago. I have it on good authority that he had a long rap sheet of both petty and violent crimes. Cross him and you might be the subject of his next police report.

The Fat Man meandered through life, looking for every opportunity to make a quick buck while staying out of jail. His lifestyle meant he was a character with plenty of outrageous stories to tell.

We met shortly after he opened a record store in my old neighborhood on the south side of Chicago. He sold mostly vinyl LPs, a few 8-track tapes that were being phased out, and the newer cassette tapes that were replacing the 8-track technology. In his store, you could also find the latest posters of all the popular rock groups or other assorted rock memorabilia. His under-the-counter inventory also included a variety of hash pipes, rolling papers, and roach clips.

My friends and I, all young single men, would frequent his store a few times a week just to see what the newest inventory looked like and because we found him to be quite entertaining.

He didn't advertise it, but if you knew The Fat Man well, he had a few lids of marijuana and perhaps some Quaaludes in the back room at a reasonable price.

Fat Man sold records cheaper than any other music store around town. As a matter of fact, myself and my friends who frequented the store could never figure out how he made money. The other record store down the street sold most albums in the 6-to-7-dollar range for a single and $12 for a double album. Fat Man sold us vinyl records for a flat $3, or $5 for a double album.

The year was 1973 (give or take). I remember the year because I got a copy of the album Bachman–Turner Overdrive II for only $3. I could sell that record today on eBay for twice what I paid.

One time, he and I were having a conversation about which music we preferred and which bands we followed. We chatted about the concerts we attended and the venues where they took place. I told him I liked Led Zeppelin, The Rolling Stones, and The Moody Blues. He told me he liked Elvis and Chuck Berry.

He commented about a band named Three Dog Night who had just released an album called Shambala, which he hated. In his words, "It is their worst album ever." He offered to sell me the album for $2 just to get it off his shelf. Sorry, no takers.

Then one day, my friends and I showed up for our usual bullshit session, but the store was closed. There was no note, no indication of a problem. Just a "Closed" sign hanging in the window.

It was about a week later before he reopened. Of course, we wanted an explanation of why he would leave us standing out on the curb with no notice. He raised up his sweatshirt and revealed the scabs from three still-healing bullet holes in his abdomen.

"What happened?" Was the collective refrain.

"I got into an argument with my wife. She put me in the hospital," he said.

Thinking she must be in jail, I asked. "Really? Where is she now?"

"Home, where she belongs. She won the argument."

We never got the full story of what happened. Being naïve twenty-year-old boys, we were all too shocked to ask any more questions. As far as I could tell, they never brought any charges against his wife. The police treated it as a run-of-the-mill domestic dispute. Typical in those days.

Cha, Cha, Cha, Changes…

It was then that The Fat Man changed his business practice. He no longer stocked the shelves with records and tapes of the latest music releases. Instead, he switched to an order-ahead business model. You simply told him which albums or tapes you wanted, and he would order them. A few days later, you could return to the store and purchase the music. Cash only, of course.

The new business model lasted only a few weeks and then one day, The Fat Man disappeared again, this time gone for good. So was our discount record store that we relied so heavily upon. But most of all, we missed the social interaction with the guy who not only gave us music but also made us laugh.

Oh, there was one other thing The Fat Man introduced us to, CRIME. As it turns out, every record that The Fat Man sold us was stolen from one of the other record stores in the neighborhood. He had an arrangement with a small group of local petty thieves that would break into other stores and steal records and tapes, then trade him for drugs or alcohol. He, in turn, would sell them to us and pocket the profits. We didn't know it at the time, but we were dealing with a criminal enterprise.

I don't know what became of The Fat Man. He probably took off to another city or town. He may have left his wife, or not. She may have finally had enough of his crap and emptied the rest of the bullets into his chest. Most likely, he continued his unscrupulous business practices in another area. Maybe the authorities finally caught up with him and he spent his days telling his wild stories to his cellmate?

This is a mostly true story. I say mostly true because, just like the characters are mostly dead, I filled in a few of the blanks. It was a long time ago and I am recalling the details from memory and my imagination. They may be a little fuzzy. When people tell me this story is all bullshit, I shrug my shoulders and say, "Maybe I got that part wrong."

Fact or fiction, it was an interesting time in my life. All I know is that I have the proof it happened. I still have several of those vinyl albums stashed in my record collection.

One album I don't have is Shambala. I never bought it. Even at a discount.

Strange things happen when you least expect them. Often a quiet night at home can lead to a memorable adventure.

Stranger Than Fiction
<u>But just as scary.</u>

I was half asleep on the couch when something stranger than fiction sent a chill through my body. I watched as a dark shadow followed across the ceiling and then disappeared into the built-in entertainment center behind the television. Special effects? A new kind of programming technique?

Startled, I peeked behind the television. There was nothing there.

"What the hell was that???" I raged.

"Just stop, it is just a shadow," my wife complained. "A bird probably flew by the window or something."

"No, it wasn't a bird. It was something, something bigger." I looked toward the window facing the rear patio. "There is something out back. I'm going out there."

Just then a clap of thunder, accompanied by a bolt of lightning, broke open the sky, illuminating the backyard landscape.

"Don't go out, it's raining. You'll get all wet. You'll make a big mess. Then I will have to clean it up," she said.

There was no stopping me. By the time I slipped my shoes on, it happened again. This time, the shadow emerged from the entertainment center and passed across the ceiling toward the door behind me. The same chill as before coursed through my body.

"Did you feel that?" I asked.

"You're imagining things. I told you not to eat the whole burrito," she said.

"It's not from the burrito."

I bolted for the back door, trying to catch the shadow before it escaped again. Turning the knob, I poked my head out into the yard. Above the sound of the rain hitting the roof, I could hear a low groaning vibration. Something was out there.

In the rain and the darkness, I couldn't see what it was, so following the sound, I trekked toward the rear of the yard. The deep groaning sound grew louder. *What the hell was it?*

Suddenly, a flash of light washed across the fence, temporarily blinding me. With the rain in my eyes and bright light blinding me, I backed away. A second flash nearly knocked me from my feet.

Then came a loud bang. It wasn't thunder but whatever it was didn't belong there. There was an uneasiness in my gut as I summoned my courage to climb back up and peek over the fence. All I could see were bright lights and a low growling machine of some type. This was getting me nowhere.

Soaked through to my skin, I made my way around the block to the street behind my house. The driving rain and bright lights only served to make the entire scene more bizarre.

"Hey, what are you doing here?" A voice from behind me yelled. "You're gonna get yourself killed."

I nearly shit my pants when I turned around to see an unrecognizable figure hovering nearby.

I snapped, "Who the hell are you?"

"I'm with the power company. This transformer is overloaded," he said. "It's going to blow. We are trying to shut it down before the entire neighborhood goes dark."

"Oh," I mumbled.

"Why are you out here?" he asked. "You better go back inside. We will alert the community when it is safe."

Relieved but still shaken up, I headed back around the block to my front door. By the time I got back inside, I was cold and shaking. My wife stood there with a smug look on her face.

"Figure it out, Sherlock?"

"You were right. It was the burrito. Now get out of my way. I need to use the bathroom. Quick."

We all have goals in life. Just when you think all your wishes have come true. You may wish for one more...

When All Your Wishes
Come True
You may want one more wish.

We had finally gotten through the traffic jam that jeopardized our on-time arrival. I hit the gas, weaving wildly in and out of traffic. Emily's voice cracked as she snapped at me over my aggressive driving. "I wish the hell you would slow down; I want to get there in one piece."

"We are not missing this plane, dammit. We have been planning this trip for years. These tickets cost a fortune. The hotel will charge us for the night, even if we are not there. Besides, we only have four days; I am not missing one of them." I replied.

As we wheeled into the airport parking lot, she commanded, "Okay, grab the first parking spot you come to."

Pointing to a spot between two oversized pickup trucks, she shouts, "There! There's one!"

"No, that one is no good. Both trucks are over the lines. I wish you would calm down."

"There, how about this one?" she said.

Pulling into the better spot, we unloaded our bags and raced to the terminal doorway. That's when we saw the line at the airport security. It weaved endlessly through a long crowd control barrier. There wasn't enough time to make it through in time.

"Damn, I wish we had Pre-check passes."

I got the attention of a security agent who was checking tickets.

"Sir, can you help? We are late for our flight. The line is too long. I'm afraid we won't make it."

The agent checked our tickets and identification, then pulled us around the line and guided us through security.

"Thank you, sir. You have been a lifesaver," I said.

As we sprinted to the gate, dodging the slow pokes, Emily exclaimed. "We're gonna make it!"

Arriving at the gate in time to grab the last two seats on the crowded plane. We plopped down, out of breath, safe, and secure, as the flight attendant closed the doors.

A few minutes later, we were airborne. Glancing outside the window, I could see our hometown disappearing behind us. After years of promising each other, we would take a break. We did it. Our wish for a romantic second honeymoon was coming true.

She reached across the aisle and took my hand. "Honey, we have had a wonderful life together," she said. "You have made all my wishes come true. I am so happy to be able to spend the rest of my life with you."

But something was wrong. The plane sputtered as it tried to gain altitude. It shook and bucked as if it were out of fuel. The cabin fell silent as the passengers all wondered what to do.

A frantic call came over the loudspeaker, "Flight attendants, assume crash positions."

I looked across the aisle at my beautiful wife, Emily. She had a tear in her eye and sadness on her face. All her wishes had come true.

"Be careful what you wish for. You just might get it.

Here's another example of strange things happening when we least expect it. In this story, our friend Walter tries to solve a problem the easy way. It doesn't turn out as he expects.

Walter And The Witch Doctor
Was it a case of mistaken identity?

Walter had to leave the birthing room. Emily would not stop screaming at the top of her lungs. It was just too much. Her overdue childbirth and long hours of painful contractions pushed both their nerves to the bitter end.

It was her 18th hour of labor, and the delivery was not going well. The baby refused to be born. The Lamaze exercises were no longer working. Epidurals weren't doing the job. The doctor refused to prescribe any additional pain medication because the risk of harming the baby was too great. He offered her a C-section, but Emily refused.

The last time Walter was in the room, she nearly choked him to death.

The hospital's staff's nerves were wearing thin as well. They offered suggestions on how to ignore the pain, but nothing more. Down in the lobby, one old man visiting the hospital lobby asked Walter, "Is that your wife I hear screaming?"

"Yes, she is in a lot of pain," he replied.

The old man proposed a solution. He knew a witch doctor who would put a spell on Emily. The spell would not harm her or the baby. If the spell works, it will transfer her pain to the child's father. She could relax until nature allows the child to be born safely.

At first, Walter refused. It was all hokum. *The old man was crazy.* He thought.

But Emily's screaming continued. Walter loved Emily; he didn't want her to suffer.

Then there was the baby. He couldn't risk something happening to the baby.

After another hour, the doctor lost patience. He gave Walter a choice. A heavy dose of sedatives for Emily and emergency surgery or the old man's spell. Walter wasn't afraid of the pain. He had been through painful episodes before. He would endure whatever was necessary to end Emily's suffering. Walter conceded to let the old man call his witch doctor friend.

It only took a few minutes for the witch doctor to arrive. To everyone's amazement, Emily stopped screaming almost immediately. Her demeanor changed. She became calm and relaxed.

Walter came back into the birthing room, and he seemed no worse for wear. Emily thought either the spell didn't work, or he must have an unusually high pain threshold.

A few hours later, a bouncing baby boy was born, the spitting image of Emily.

Walter never flinched. He never felt any pain. It seemed all was right with the world.

About thirty minutes later, Walter's phone rang. It was his sister-in-law. He announced the good news. "It's a boy!"

"That's wonderful. Congratulations," she said. "But there is something else."

Then, she broke the bad news to Walter that they had rushed his twin brother Bobby to the hospital. "He just doubled over in pain. The doctors haven't been able to diagnose his problem."

When two people search for a soul mate the attraction to someone with the same values can be appealing. For Benny and Clarice their comfort zone was a bit too small.

Too Close For Comfort
The story of Benny and Clarice.

Each morning Benny watched through the glass wall that divided their offices as Clarice dashed past on her way to the elevator. Some days, when she wasn't in a hurry, she would wave and smile through the glass partition.

If she had extra time, she would peek her head inside the big glass door and say, "Good morning, Benny, how are you today?"

Other days, she moved so fast he couldn't get her attention. She didn't notice him waiting for her to pass by and acknowledge him.

Benny had grown extremely fond of Clarice ever since they had met weeks ago. Everyone could see he was infatuated with her, and she seemed to crave his attention in the same way.

It was one-day last month when the two strangers became friends at the corporate biannual sales event. Benny had taken his seat in the 3rd row right behind the executive officers. His recent promotion to group manager warranted a spot near the front of the auditorium. Being visible to the upper management was a perk that was going to help his career over the next few months.

Clarice was late arriving at the event. She was stuck on a sales call with a big client and a chance for a bigger-than-normal order. By the time she entered the auditorium, all the seats in the section where her co-workers sat had been filled. There were two open seats next to Benny. He waved his hand and invited Clarice to join him.

After a brief introduction, they found themselves to have a lot in common. Benny had started his career in the same department as Clarice, so he knew some of her co-workers and how she did her job.

Clarice, although not unhappy with her current position, hoped one day to advance to a management position. Sitting in the 3rd row would not hurt her visibility.

Benny liked Clarice the moment she sat down next to him. Her irrepressible smile and easy-going attitude captivated him each time he saw her. She seemed to possess a familiarity that gave him comfort. Clarice felt the same simpatico presence whenever they were together.

Shortly after that meeting, Benny would go out of his way to bump into Clarice. One time when they met in the elevator, Benny stood so close to her that he could smell the fragrant perfume she wore. When he reached down and accidentally touched her hand, she didn't pull away. There was a feeling of electricity that flowed between them when they were together.

As the other occupants exited the elevator, Benny saw his chance. He turned toward Clarice and looked directly into her eyes. Her wanton look was all he needed. He was going for broke. He leaned in for a first kiss. Clarice closed her eyes, anticipating his warm lips against hers. He was only inches away when the elevator stopped. The doors opened, and two executives stepped in to join them. Benny backed away. The company frowned on interoffice relationships. He was okay for now, but he missed his chance.

Before they returned to their respective offices, Benny asked Clarice to have lunch the next day. It would be their first chance to be alone together, away from the prying eyes at their work. She cheerfully accepted. It seemed it was full steam ahead for their budding romance.

But the next day she had to cancel when her young son came down with a fever and could not go to school or daycare. Clarice asked Benny for a raincheck, leaving their status in limbo for the time being.

But for some reason, the lunch never got rescheduled. Time and again, he wanted to remind her of his invitation, but didn't want to appear needy. After all, it was her that canceled the first time.

The botched lunch date bothered Clarice as well. She worried her cancellation sent the wrong message. She wanted to jog his memory again without asking him directly. Today was the day. She decided to buttonhole him again for a quick conversation.

She found Benny, alone, waiting in the lobby for one of his team members. But before she could catch his attention, another young woman approached him and greeted him with a hug. The two shared a laugh and then made their way down the hall toward Benny's office.

"Drat," she mumbled. "Bad timing." She headed upstairs to her desk. Their chance meeting would have to wait.

Like two ships passing in the night, Benny and Clarice appeared to be on different courses.

As soon as Benny concluded his business with the first woman, he sat back in his chair, pondering his next move with Clarice. Enough was enough. He jumped up from his seat, marched upstairs to Clarice's desk, and boldly reminded her she agreed to lunch with him.

Over the moon, Clarice agreed, once again apologizing for the first cancellation.

Each of the two would-be lovers waited with bated breath for their first real opportunity to begin a relationship. One that could become a storybook romance if all went well.

Each one worried about how the lunch would go. Benny worried that Clarice might wonder why a man nearly forty years old has never married. Clarice worried Benny might look at her previous failed marriage and single mother status as a difficult situation to overcome.

Still, they were too much alike not to be enamored with each other.

Over lunch, they both realized they barely knew each other. It was as if they were introducing themselves again for the first time. They played twenty questions, trying to learn more about the person across the table that had them so infatuated.

The lunch went better than expected, each one keeping the other delighted with their life stories.

When Benny reached across the table and took Clarice's hand, their collective hearts began to pound with anticipation. To Benny, she was everything he could want in a woman. Smart, funny, attractive, she had it all. He wasn't concerned that she had a school-aged child. He would make every effort to show the boy he was not stealing his mother away.

All was going well in their budding relationship. On the way back to the office, they held hands.

It wasn't until Clarice revealed that her mother grew up in Juddville, a small town a few hours away, that Benny became concerned. It didn't make sense. Benny was born in Juddville and lived there until he was 12 years old. His family moved to the city for his father's job. He knew many people in Juddville and no one with Clarice's last name.

The population of Juddville was only a few hundred people. So small their families must know each other. Clarice agreed and asked more about his family. When Benny revealed his mother's maiden name was Shuman, Clarice became alarmed.

Benny wrapped his arm around her waist, once again attempting to garner that first kiss. This time, Clarice pushed him away. Benny's revelation suddenly made sense to her.

"No!" she exclaimed. "Benny we can't."

Confused, Benny cried, "Clarice, can't you see how much I like you?"

"Benny, my mom's maiden name is also Shuman. My mom and your mom are sisters. You are my first cousin."

The revelation shocked Benny. He pondered it for a few seconds, then took a step back, realizing what she said.

They looked back at each other and in unison, they both exclaimed, "EEEEEWWW!"

"Hey, Buzz. Two more…"
<u>The usual, please.</u>

"Is that Tommy, I see?"

"Howdy Ned, it has been a long time. Mind if I join ya?"

"Have a seat ol' buddy."

Ned called out to the bartender. "Hey, Buzz. Set up a couple for me and my buddy Tommy here. The usual, two tappers and two shots of rye."

"So, where have you been?"

"I haven't been able to come this way in a while. I just got my driver's license back. Suspended three months. Some BS about being over the limit. I don't know how that could be. I always drink the same thing. A couple of beers and a couple of shots, then I head home."

"That sucks."

"Yeah, it was some new deputy I had never seen before. Trying to make Sergeant I guess."

"Yeah, I know what you mean. The other day I was burning trash on that property up there by the highway. One of those A-holes at the new grocery store called the fire department. They said I was polluting the air. I have been burning trash at that spot for twenty-five years. It never polluted the air until now."

"I know, too many goddam rules nowadays. Too much government interference. I used to dump all my old fertilizers and used motor oil in the stream behind my land. Now they tell me I can't do that anymore. It never bothered anyone before."

"That's nothing. I had a guy from the EPA come by my property about two weeks ago. You know those three acres where I buried the old cars? He fined me and now I have to dig them up. Fucking bureaucrats, I say."

"Yeah, a couple of months ago they started building that new subdivision off of Parker Rd. They put up two stop signs on the corner. I have been going that way for thirty years and never had to stop. I got pissed and took the signs down. Then two days ago there was a terrible accident right there on that corner. They airlifted the people to the hospital in town. In thirty years, there was never an accident. The county puts up two stop signs and people start getting killed."

"Hey, Buzz. Another round for my buddy Tommy and me."

"Yeah Ned, it's Socialism I tell ya. They want to control everything. Got any cigarettes?"

"Yes, but you can't smoke in here anymore. You gotta go stand outside in the cold. More bullshit rules."

"What the hell is happening in this great country of ours? They are stealing our freedom a little at a time. I was out shooting my gun in the yard the other day and a bullet ricocheted off a rock and damaged a delivery truck going by. Now the FedEx guy won't come to my house anymore."

"Yeah, that sucks. Want another one?"

"Yeah, just one or two more, then I gotta go. The cops set up those DUI checkpoints on Saturday night. I can't get stopped again."

"Just drive with your lights off. They won't see you."

"Good idea, I'll try it. Hey Buzz. Two more…"

Everyone enjoys steamy noir mysteries (at least I do). In this tale of mystery, there are many factors at play. How will it turn out?

Mrs. Fairbang
The woman in the red dress.

She had everything. Long legs that stretched all the way from the soles of her shoes to a place that looked like a page from Hustler magazine. Her hourglass figure reminded me of old Hollywood stars, like Marilyn Monroe or Jane Mansfield. Her waist was so small compared to her hips and chest that logic told you it was in defiance of the laws of nature. The only thing that separated her from the 1950s was her modern short haircut, which looked more like something you would see on a girl in a hip-hop video.

I couldn't tell her age at first. Her face said mid-twenties, her figure thirty-five. Her dark hair with a couple of streaks of translucent green reminded me of a runaway teenage girl. But it was her clothes that almost threw me for a loop. She wore a tight red silk dress that clung to her skin, revealing two perfectly shaped breasts that held their own without a bra. The slit at the side showed as much of those long legs as possible without getting her arrested. Draped over her shoulders, she wore what looked like an ermine stole. An accessory that is out of character for a young woman today.

She completed the entire ensemble with gaudy jewelry. A diamond necklace and matching earrings contrasted nicely with her tan-all-over skin tone. Clasped around her wrist hung a platinum bracelet so large it must have made it hard for her to raise her arm. Wrapped on the finger of her left hand was a ring that could easily be mistaken for Elizabeth Taylor's Krupp Diamond. If those stones were real, they would be worth a fortune.

It was her voice that sealed the deal. Not bubbly like a valley girl, but deep and sultry, almost erotic. She was seated ten feet across the room, but when she spoke, it was like she was whispering in my ear. It was enough to make a man's blood rush from his brain to other parts of his body that he didn't control as well.

She wanted to be free of her abusive husband. She came to me because of my reputation as a man who gets things done.

I watched her lips move and could hear words coming from her mouth. The words meant nothing. All I could concentrate on were her breasts heaving up and down as she spoke. When she paused to confirm my understanding, I nodded my head in agreement.

"Good, come to my house tonight after 10:00 p.m. We can discuss the details over a bottle of French Champagne." She handed me a card with her address.

As she turned toward the door, she dropped her car keys. "Oops", she chirped. Then she bent over to pick them up, proudly displaying her shapely leg, covered by a silk stocking, held up by a black garter belt. My heart skipped a beat.

I would do anything to help bring to an end her unhappy situation. Anything she asked.

At 9:45 p.m. I opened my desk drawer and poured myself a shot of 12-year-old Irish Whisky. I needed my ounce of courage.

I slid my gun into its holster, hoisted my gray trench coat from its hook by the door, and locked the office door behind me.

In less than one hour, that red dress will be lying on her bedroom floor. I intend to show her how a real man should treat a woman.

We will spend the night together. By tomorrow morning, she will be the former Mrs. Fairbang.

Here's a story of a man who was going nowhere, FAST.

The Blue Phallic Symbol
<u>He kept hitting the gas.</u>

I live in a semi-rural area, just outside of Scottsdale, Arizona. The long distance to the city center means I spend a lot of time driving. Almost daily, I drive to the grocery store, coffee shop, or restaurant. Each trip can easily be ten miles, often longer. In the winter, we experience the snowbird phenomenon, where the population doubles for several months. The roadways don't support the additional visitors very well, so traffic can be irritating. Sometimes it drives you crazy.

The other day I was on a busy roadway that acts as a feeder to the interstate highway. Most of the drivers on the road were just trying to make their way through traffic without a collision or road rage incident. The latter being the more difficult to avoid.

Wouldn't you know it, there was one idiot who refused to keep pace with the rest of us. He drove a blue late model sports car. Like a lot of auto aficionados, he had modified his car by removing the factory mufflers and replacing them with ones that blast a loud rumble whenever he hit the gas. And hit the gas he did, about every ten seconds. He would hit the gas, race up to the bumper of the car in front of him, then brake using a low gear further bellowing a loud reverberation. There was no reason for his actions other than to attract attention to himself and his bright blue car. Each time he did, it was as if he was screaming, "Look at Me! Look at Me!"

I never understood why people have to use a machine to illustrate their importance. It makes me wonder, *What are they compensating for?* As a man who is fully confident in my own presence, I do not find the need to continuously call attention to myself. The man, or boy, behind the wheel of this blue boner, could only satisfy his existence if everyone was looking at him.

It is a common occurrence. I got into an argument with an old friend over something similar. In this case, it was his penchant for loud motorcycles. I like motorcycles as well as anyone. I used to ride when I was younger and admit it was fun. But I never understood why some riders have to sit in traffic revving their engines, for no reason. Calling attention to themselves and their formidable engine.

Once, my brother-in-law tried to shame me by saying that I was afraid to ride powerful motorcycles. He implied I was not man enough. Well, I would not give him satisfaction, but in some ways, he was correct. I am fearful of riding a bike in heavy city traffic. There are just too many bad drivers on the road to contend with. I prefer the comfort and quiet of my luxury car.

I was able to put an end to the conversation by replying. "I don't need a big, powerful bike to prove I am a man. I was born with a big, powerful dick." My comment struck a nerve. The remark angered him so badly that he left the table, went outside, climbed on his Harley, and revving his engine as loudly as he could, rumbled off. A few weeks later, my sister informed me I was out of their will.

Getting back to my nemesis with the blue sports car. Apparently, he thought his car and his wild driving made him the envy of every other car on the road.

He kept up his antics for several miles. Racing his engine. Speeding up ahead of other cars, then getting stopped by a traffic light or another car turning in front of him. He switched lanes time and again, trying to make his way through traffic, all the while making a commotion and frustrating himself.

As we approached the Interstate, the traffic eased a little, and I was able to find an open lane that moved at a steady pace. In seconds I had caught up to my friend in the blue phallic symbol. When in his haste he got in the wrong turning lane, he ended up having to wait as a dozen other cars turned in front of him. He watched as I passed him, heading for the highway. No amount of engine revving or peeling out was going to get him onto the Interstate ramp before me.

I gave him a one finger wave as I cruised silently past him. My bigger dick was now quite evident. I laughed as his blue boner went limp right there in the middle of a traffic jam.

Doing stupid things seems to be a pre-requisite to adulthood. Sometimes mistakes are costly or last a lifetime. Other times they just make a memorable story.

Saturday Night Party Fail
–Circa 1972
<u>It was going to be legendary.</u>

It was going to be a night out discovering new hangouts, meeting new friends, and for my buddy Cary and me, a chance to see how the other half lives. So, Saturday evening, Cary and I climbed into his 1970 yellow Dodge Challenger and headed out from our working-class neighborhood on the Southside Chicago.

Our destination was the far north suburb of Evanston, IL — home to the upscale business executives and high-paid doctors and lawyers of the metro area. Cary had a friend who lived up there and invited him to hang out and party with his friends. It was to be an unforgettable Saturday evening.

Our route took us into the city center, across downtown, and heading north up Interstate 90, a busy four-lane highway, toward the north shore of Lake Michigan — a distance of about forty miles. We were still about ten miles from our destination when the skies opened up and the rain poured down in buckets, cutting visibility and flooding the low spots on the roadway.

Despite the wet roads, Cary was in a hurry. He continued to drive aggressively, weaving in and out of traffic and passing slower cars, delivery trucks, and taxicabs. As he tried to merge into a right lane to pass another car, one of the slower drivers cut in front of him. Cary hit the brakes, a big mistake considering the slippery conditions of the road surface.

The car began to slide and swerve. Cary tried to correct his way out of the slide by steering into the slide, but the car lost traction and went into an uncontrollable spin. I grabbed the dashboard to brace myself for the inevitable crash. At seventy-plus miles per hour, I thought we were sure to meet our maker.

We spun three-hundred-sixty degrees, over and over, as my life passed before my eyes. It was a miracle that no other car crashed into us.

Then, magically, the rear wheels regained traction. The car righted itself temporarily, accelerated, and then catapulted us toward the center island that divided the north and southbound lanes of the Interstate.

We slammed into the six-inch high concrete curbing, flew several feet into the air, and skidded to a halt in the grassy center aisle. The car slapped down with the wheels partially buried in the mud.

We climbed out of the car and glanced around as the traffic continued to speed by us at high speed. We looked at each other, amazed that we had both escaped unscathed.

The car was not so lucky. The impact from hitting the curb blew out both front tires, and it looked as if the rim of the driver's side rear had been bent in the crash.

We were in trouble, and we knew it. If we didn't act fast, a police car would come along and likely give Cary a ticket and call for a city tow truck to pull our car from the mud.

Having the car towed to a city lot would be costly and inconvenient. Likewise, the cost of towing the car back forty miles to our neighborhood was out of the question. But as luck would have it, just off the expressway a few hundred feet ahead was a gas station/garage. It looked like they had a tow truck.

We crossed over the expressway, avoiding the traffic, and walked down the ramp to get help. The garage owner must have felt sorry for us because he agreed to pull Cary's car off the expressway and to his lot where he could repair the car.

In fifteen minutes, the tow truck driver was hoisting Cary's Challenger onto the bed of the recovery vehicle.

After getting the car to his lot, the garage owner determined it would cost several hundred dollars to replace the two tires, rebalance and realign the wheels, and use Cary's spare to replace the bent rear wheel. Being Saturday evening, he wouldn't be able to get the parts until Monday. He suggested we leave the car there and come back when it was repaired.

Cary had a plan "B". We could go back home, get his spare snow tires from his dad's garage, and use those to replace the two-blown tires. The other rim was bent, but Cary had a spare that would suffice if we drove the car slowly back home, where he could execute more permanent repairs for hundreds less than the garage wanted.

We called a cab to take us back home. The cost of a taxi ride of forty miles would be more than one hundred dollars. We didn't have that much cash, so we moved on to plan "C".

We had the taxi drive us to the elevated train station about two miles away. We then rode the train to downtown Chicago, another five miles. Then took a city bus from downtown back to our neighborhood.

Once back home, we had to load the two snow tires into my car. But my car was a late-model Camaro, with a very small trunk. The two spare tires would not fit. So, we slipped one tire as far as it would go into the trunk and tied the trunk closed. We wedged the other wheel and tire into my back seat.

It was nearly 9:00 p.m. when we headed back up north, again repeating our forty-mile trek across the city up toward the north burbs.

Fortunately, the garage stayed open late on weekends. We arrived back at about 10:00 p.m.

In the garage parking lot, we swapped out the two front-blown tires, then took the wheel with the bent rim and traded it with Cary's spare tire from his trunk. By 11:00 p.m. the car was somewhat road-worthy again.

I followed Cary as we drove home slowly, using the surface streets and avoiding the interstate. The route took longer, but we were not willing to risk another breakdown at high speed.

It was after midnight when we arrived back at Cary's house, exhausted.

We never made it up to Evanston to hang out with Cary's friend for our legendary Saturday evening. Instead, we had one of the craziest and most memorable experiences of our youth.

Everyone deserves to have a happy holiday season. For Karen, times were tough. If only the spirit of Christmas could somehow find a way to save the day.

Clean Clothes For Christmas
<u>She needed a second chance.</u>

Karen struggled to push the shopping cart through the early-season snow that coated the sidewalk. "Damn, why can't they shovel better?" she grumbled.

The heavy white stuff falling all around sent a chill through her body and threatened to ruin the last remains of her belongings. She had to find a place to escape the squall, at least for a few hours.

Up ahead, she spied an overpass and what looked like a cavity she could squat under for a while.

Karen considered herself lucky. She had convinced her Aunt Millie to care for her young son. Despite the already overcrowded situation at Millie's apartment, she agreed to let Kyle stay there while Karen worked odd jobs in an effort to work her way out of the misery caused by the failure of society to support one another.

For the last two years, Christmas was a foreign concept for Karen. Evicted when she lost her job, the street was her home now. Unless something changed, there would be no Christmas again this year.

But she had a plan. More businesses were hiring holiday help. A few weeks of steady work and she would be able to buy a used mini-van. She could start her rideshare business and she won't have to sleep in a tent or on the street any longer.

The mini-van was her first priority, but with the holidays fast approaching, she needed to find a Christmas present for Kyle. Karen could not stand to see the sadness on his face again this year.

As she passed by the neighborhood department store, she spotted a toy fire truck. It looked so real with flexible hoses, a working siren, and flashing lights. It was the perfect Christmas gift for Kyle. She imagined the smile on his face when he unwrapped the box at Aunt Millie's on Christmas morning.

Karen promised herself as soon as she got her paycheck this Friday, she would come back and buy the truck on layaway. If all went well, she would have the toy paid for in time to put it under Aunt Millie's tree.

As she pushed the cart up the incline under the overpass, she searched for a dry spot out of the wind. It would be her hovel for the next few hours until she could start her 4-hour shift at the fast-food restaurant around the corner. She looked forward to work because it was warm inside and although against company policy, she could get a bite to eat. Store policy required her to throw away any food that a customer returned or rejected. Most of the time, there was nothing wrong with it. She could hide the sandwich or burger in her bag until her bathroom break.

As the snow pummeled down harder, Karen sat shivering. There was nowhere for her to go. She had worn out her welcome at the local shops and restaurants that didn't want penniless people scaring off paying customers. She understood. Times were tough for everyone. Even those with successful businesses feared the worst, nervous about their future in a changing world.

She envied the wealthy people who strolled through the shopping malls and department stores listening to Christmas carols and planning their turkey dinners and pumpkin pies. While Karen and others like her battled the elements and struggled with rising costs and low pay. To her, it seemed the promise of The Great Society had been abandoned in favor of the failed Trickle-Down Economy.

Even so, it would soon be Christmas. Surely mankind would find a way once again to come together and find a common ground? Surely Kris Kringle, Old Saint Nick or Santa Claus, whatever you call him, will find a way to bring joy and laughter to everyone big and small, rich and poor?

When she spotted the clock on the wall of the bank across the street, she was relieved to see it was almost 4:00 p.m. In a few minutes, she could start her shift at the sandwich shop. Nearly half frozen, she welcomed the chance to have some feeling back in her fingers and toes. With any luck, her supervisor will let her park the shopping cart under the canopy of the receiving area, out of the snow, and away from anyone who might want to help themselves to her belongings.

She nearly slipped and fell on the snow-covered embankment as she climbed down from under the overpass. But the cart got away from her and rolled precariously into the street in front of an oncoming car.

Karen rushed to pull it out of the way. She couldn't risk causing damage to someone else's car and certainly could not afford to lose all of her belongings.

When the car stopped, and the driver climbed out, Karen prepared herself for a confrontation. It wouldn't be the first time someone assaulted a down-and-out resident of the streets. One time, a few weeks ago, an older man pulled a gun on her and screamed profanities at her while she slinked away in fear.

But this time it was different. The man, tall and slender, did not seem angry. He was handsome, with a professional aura about him. Karen guessed by the look of his new expensive red SUV, he had money. More than most.

"Are you all right?" he asked.

"Yes, I will be out of your way in a minute," she replied.

"Where are you going?"

"I am on my way to work at the sandwich shop around the corner."

"Anything I can do?" he asked.

"No, I will be fine," came the reply.

Karen pulled her cart around the corner as the man watched. Happy, she avoided the hostility that often comes from dealing with those who do not understand her situation.

In a minute, she would be safe and warm inside her place of work for a few hours.

For the rest of the afternoon, work was typical. It was slow at the beginning, with business building up as it grew closer to the dinner hour. The drive-thru window seemed to be busier today than normal as fewer and fewer people came into the store to order their food.

Around 6:00 p.m., Karen noticed her boss having a discussion with one of the customers. It was the man from the SUV, her earlier encounter on the street. He was talking with her supervisor, then motioned toward Karen.

"Shit," she mumbled. "This guy is going to cause trouble. I can't afford to lose this job."

She put her head down and continued to service the drive-thru window, hoping for the best.

"Karen," called her boss. "Could you please come over here?"

That was it. She could feel something was going on. "I haven't done anything wrong," she protested.

The stranger interjected. "No, you haven't. I just need to speak with you for a minute."

Her boss returned to the counter, while Karen took a seat across from the man in the dining room.

"About our meeting earlier," he said. "I want you to know that when I asked you if there was anything I could do, I meant it. I can see you are having a tough time. If you let me, I would like to help."

"I don't need your charity; I need a chance. I need a good job and a place for me and my son to live. That's all I need."

He handed her a business card. "I own a string of laundromats in the city. I need a maintenance person. Your tasks will include cleaning up spills, emptying lint traps, and stocking the vending machines. It is not a glamorous job, and it's hard work, but I can pay you more than you get here, a lot more. If you are willing to take on some responsibility. You can set your own schedule, as long as you service every location once a day."

"I don't have a car right now. How will I get to the stores?"

"I have a mini-van that I use for company business. You can use it for work and occasionally for personal errands if you keep it to a minimum. You can start next week if you like," he said.

Karen could not believe her ears. With the higher pay, she will be able to rent an apartment for herself and Kyle. They would be a family again, with a home for the holidays.

This was the greatest Christmas present she could ever imagine.

"Okay, it's a deal," she said.

Karen looked at the name on his business card. This couldn't be right. She rubbed her eyes and looked again. To her amazement, her new boss's name was written in bold letters.

"Nick St. Kringle — President Claus Enterprises"

Going to a casino can be fun and rewarding. With more than just gambling, our two friends Tom and Gary take an evening to explore their options. They discover there is more than one way to be a winner.

A Night At The Casino
How Tom and Gary became winners.

Two friends Tom and Gary, both in their mid-twenties, decided it was time to break away from their usual in-home video games and try something with a higher risk/reward. Tom suggested a nearby casino. There they could gamble a few bucks, have dinner at one of the casino's upscale restaurants, and walk away winners.

He called it a night of Stake and Steak.

Gary agreed and the next evening they showered, shaved, and put on clean button-down shirts.

Off they went to the land of make-believe for a night on the town. The casino was a classy-looking building with bright lights and a huge circle driveway that led to large glass doors. Behind the main building, the complex included a labyrinth of retail stores, restaurants, and a conference center/hotel.

The television commercials for this casino all showed handsome, James Bond-type actors, dressed in classy tuxedos and holding an expensive cocktail in one hand and a stack of betting chips in the other.

The women were portrayed as sexy starlets in sequined party dresses and high heels. Their girl next door gleam polluted by an "I feel like being bad tonight" look of a temptress.

Tom and Gary couldn't wait for their night of hobnobbing with the trendy celebrities of the day.

Once they stepped inside, they were disappointed to see the image portrayed by the TV ads was greatly overblown.

Most of the people were dressed in T-shirts and blue jeans. Some looked like Hip-Hop wannabes, others like street people. One older woman who had staked her position at a "Wheel of Fortune" machine looked nothing like the vixens on the television. The woman, well into her seventies, was a balding, wrinkled, feeble-looking creature. Her hair was dyed an unnatural-looking brown color, her lipstick a blatant red to match her fingernails.

She had the slot machine's pull lever firmly grasped in her right hand; her left holding a watered-down cocktail and a cigarette dangling from her lips.

Gary looked around for the beautiful young woman he saw in the TV commercial, but she was nowhere to be found. In the seat where James Bond was supposed to be seated was a construction worker in a flannel shirt and John Deere baseball cap.

Undaunted, Tom suggested, "Let's see if we can win enough money to pay for our dinner." They both agreed to keep their betting amount to a fifty-dollar maximum.

Gary nodded in agreement, so they each found a machine they thought was ready to pay out. Tom chose a video poker machine. Gary spotted a slot machine just down the aisle from the smoking lady. He thought she might have an insight into where the good machines were located.

In about a half hour, a frustrated Gary appeared behind Tom. "I lost all my money."

Tom replied, "I have three dollars left. This next draw is my last chance to win."

A few seconds later, their run at the casino's progressive jackpot was over.

"Come on, let's get some dinner before we head home," Tom offered.

They found a nice steakhouse restaurant at the back of the casino strategically hidden so that every patron would have to walk through the entire casino to find it. The restaurant was crowded, and the maître d' informed them the wait would be about forty-five minutes for a table. With nowhere else to go, Gary put their name on the list and waited for a table.

Two older women arrived a few minutes later. They had a reservation, so they were seated immediately at a four-top table in the corner. Tom and Gary huddled near the doorway, trying to stay out of the way.

After a few minutes, one of the ladies from the four-top table came over and invited Tom and Gary to join them.

The women, both well into their sixties, were attractive and well-dressed. They introduced themselves as Estelle and Helen. Helen, a former nurse, and Estelle, a retired high-school principal, were visitors from out of town.

"We enjoy traveling together," explained Estelle. "We are looking forward to our next grand adventure. Do you guys like adventure?"

"Of course," replied Tom. "Who doesn't?"

At first, Tom and Gary thought it would be a pleasant dinner with two new acquaintances. When the women offered to pay for dinner, Tom grew a little apprehensive, but he agreed. The women plied them with drinks, bought them prime steaks, and shared sumptuous desserts with the men. It was an unfamiliar experience for them. They hadn't seen anything in the TV commercial about this type of adventure.

After paying the check, Estelle took Gary's hand, "Come on young man, I want to show you how to be a winner in this casino."

As they exited the restaurant, Tom saw Gary up ahead, arm in arm, with Estelle heading across the casino toward the hotel elevator.

"I guess it's just you and me," Helen teased.

"I think I am going to need another drink," Gary replied.

"Don't worry, I have plenty of liquor in my room," she answered.

Sometimes we wait too long for happiness. Other times we wait just long enough.

What's A Nice Girl Like You Doing In A Place Like This

<u>He knew her from somewhere.</u>

Bryan had heard of men they call incels. Those men who chose celibacy. He never considered himself to be abstinent, even though he hadn't been in a romantic relationship in nearly twenty years. He just never had time. It wasn't important. "I'll meet someone someday," he would say to anyone who asked.

When his sister reminded him how long it had been, he agreed it was time to get out there and find a partner. *But where to start?*

Some of the salesmen at work spoke about a high-end club near the airport. Ben, a self-proclaimed ladies' man, said, "The girls at Bachelor's Cove are really friendly". *What did he have to lose?*

The next evening, he showered, shaved, and styled his hair. He donned his tailored light gray Hugo Boss suit and blended it with a dark blue Murano necktie. After polishing his shoes and splashing on a generous portion of Bleu de Chanel cologne, Bryan was ready to meet his future.

Bachelor's Cove wasn't what he expected. The women bartenders, servers, and dancers were all half-naked. Ben called it a gentleman's club, but the way the men were acting was anything but gentlemanly. The customers were almost all older businessmen dressed in grey or blue business suits and colorful Jerry Garcia neckties. They drank hard liquor, smoked cigars, and tempted the dancers with fists full of five and ten-dollar bills.

Within seconds of sitting at a table just a few feet from the stage, a petite young hottie with short dark hair and alabaster skin appeared. Her voice dripped like honey from a beehive, when she asked, "What can I get you, doll?" Bryan ordered a light beer and watched her shimmy away towards the bar to get his drink. Bryan turned his attention to the stage.

The first dancer, a redhead named Tawny, was finishing up her act. She had a dozen five and ten-dollar bills tucked into her G-string and another pile of bills on the floor at her feet. It must have totaled two hundred bucks. When the music stopped, Tawny collected her bounty and waved goodbye to her admirers. *Not bad for ten minutes of work.*

The stage went dark for a few minutes until a tall, slender blonde stepped forward. She wore a tight silver chiffon party dress. Not as shapely as Tawny, she appeared quite a few years older than the other girls in the room. She wasn't a dancer but introduced herself as Toni, the manager. An attractive woman in her own right, she took on the persona of an emcee.

She queried the audience with questions like, "Are you having a good time?", and "Did Tawny get your motor running?".

The blonde did a short comedy skit of five or six jokes, then followed up with a reminder that for the next ten minutes, all drinks would be two dollars off. "So, drink up, enjoy yourself."

Although she tried to direct her comments to the entire audience, her eyes locked onto Bryan. She stammered for a second, as if she knew him. Bryan recognized her too. He didn't know where, but he was sure they had met before.

Toni introduced the next dancer, but before she left the stage, she glanced back and blew a kiss towards Bryan. Her boldness towards him elicited hoots and hollers from the drunks at the table in front of him. Bryan ignored them but was intrigued by the attention she directed his way.

A few seconds later the music blared, the lights flashed, and a sexy Latina girl bounced onto the stage. Angel had a face that matched her name. Her body told a different story. Her voluptuousness brought the men at the table to his left, to their feet. They clambered to slip their hands full of greenbacks into her G-string and bikini top.

One gray-haired man in a tailored silk suit stood up and waved a fifty-dollar bill at her. Angel responded by dropping her top, revealing two perfectly formed teardrop-shaped breasts. The crowd cheered, and the man tossed the fifty on the stage.

It shocked Bryan to see how much money these horny old men were wasting on an amateur show. It was bad enough that he paid six dollars for a beer. He wasn't going to toss ten or fifteen dollars away just to see some girl flash her breasts.

He had come to Bachelor's Cove to meet someone, but this wasn't at all what he had in mind. Bryan finished his beer, dropped ten dollars on the table, more than enough to cover his bill, and walked toward the door.

On his way out, he nodded to the bouncer, a big guy with a beard and tattoos on both arms.

As he stepped outside, he noticed his blonde admirer near the door, smoking a cigarette. She waved him over. "Your name's Bryan, isn't it?"

"Sorry, I know we've met, but I can't place you," he replied.

"I'm not surprised you don't recognize me; it's been a long time. You probably remember me as Tony Carter. From Central High School."

Bryan couldn't believe his eyes. "Tony, I hardly recognized you."

She smiled. "Yes, I spell it T-O-N-I now."

Bryan paused, looking Toni up and down. "Wow, you look amazing. Have you changed? I mean completely?"

"Yes, for five years. I am just as much a woman as those dancers you've been watching on stage. I am so much happier these days."

"I didn't know. My god, you're beautiful."

"Thank you, and you're as handsome as ever. It was nice seeing you again."

Bryan turned toward the parking lot. He was still in shock.

Before he could get more than a few yards away, Toni called out. "Bryan, if you would like to get together sometime, maybe for coffee or a drink? Call me." She handed him a card with her name and number.

Bryan slipped the card into his pocket.

All the way home, he couldn't get Toni out of his mind. It wasn't just that she was beautiful. He felt something. A connection he had never felt before. It was confusing.

The next few days, everywhere he looked, at work, at the gym, at the coffee shop, all he saw were people with partners. They had husbands, wives, girlfriends, boyfriends, mistresses. Even Leonard, the short fat gay security guard, was married. Why not me? He wondered.

Tired of being the only one who stayed home alone night after night, week after week, he grabbed his phone and dialed.

Bryan made his choice. He was going to break his period of celibacy. Toni or Tony, it didn't matter. No one would call him incel again.

Staying out of trouble as a teenager wasn't always easy. The challenge was to find places that welcomed you. My friends and I found a few. This story is about one of those places.

The Beanery
<u>One of those places I will never forget.</u>

It was an out-of-the-way place in my hometown of Chicago. At the back of the railroad yard, a couple of rundown buildings stood near the end of a dirt road. They were little more than shacks, with faded grey wood siding and dirty windows. At first glance, it looked like a strong wind could blow them over. Despite that, they stood there for over fifty years.

Three of the buildings were rooming houses where the transient railroad workers could bed down for a night or two. Some stayed longer if they found a job that kept them in town. Some workers with skills, like welders and machinists, were always in demand.

This little nabe was a relic of the old days when the railroads dominated transportation. As a small boy, my friends and I rode our bicycles past the place, on our daytime adventures.

In the largest of the buildings was a dining hall. The railroad maintained the kitchen, which they called The Beanery, as a benefit for the workers. Beaneries were common in railroad yards across the country.

The Beanery, with its Old Dutch soda sign in front and big Royal Crown Cola thermometer on the wall, appeared to be lost in time. In the glass pane on the front door hung a cardboard sign that read Open or Closed. The irregular hours depended on the time of day or how many railroad men worked that day.

We never went inside until I grew up to be a teenager. That's when I learned The Beanery didn't only serve railroad workers; they were open to the public. Anyone who had cash could eat there. At first, I wasn't sure why anyone would want to eat with a bunch of hobos and drifters. I soon discovered why it was a good place to visit.

Around my 16th or 17th birthday, my buddies and I discovered we liked to drink beer and cheap wine. We hung out wherever we could to stay out of trouble. On the street corner, in an alley, or in someone's garage, if it was available. The legal age for drinking was twenty-one, so every time we took a sip of whatever illicit beverage, we were able to scrounge up, we were breaking the law.

Winter's arrival made standing on the street corner or huddling in the alley unbearable. We couldn't go to the neighborhood restaurants or shops. After a few beers, no respectable business wanted a bunch of drunk teenagers hanging around. The men at The Beanery didn't care. As long as we didn't break anything or start a fight, we were welcome to sit and talk.

The dining room had stark furnishings, including a couple of wooden tables and a U-shaped counter that could seat about 20 people. Behind the counter stood a rudimentary kitchen, where the cook prepared the meals for the railroad workers and transients who worked as day laborers.

As the trains pulled in and out of the yard, transient men from across the country would disembark. Others would climb aboard on their way to the next town. Clarence was one of those transients.

He rolled into Chicago in an empty boxcar nearly four years earlier. Clarence had spent time in every "Podunk" town from Albuquerque to Milwaukee. A few weeks here, a few days there. This Beanery was the first place he called home since he ran away from an abusive father at fourteen years old.

A small man with thinning gray hair and leathery skin, Clarence looked like the quintessential hobo. He always seemed to be wearing the same grey pinstriped pants and an old, faded sweatshirt, complete with food stains. He wore suspenders to keep his pants, which hung below his pot belly from falling down. When he smiled, the few remaining green teeth revealed a lifetime of missing dental care. Yet, he was comfortable in his own skin, having no one to impress.

On the road most of his life, he did every job from dishwasher to ditch digger. Now a short-order cook, he could whip up the best cinnamon raisin oatmeal for breakfast or a steaming bowl of spicy chili for lunch. Although strictly against railroad policy, Clarence kept a bottle of sour mash in his bag tucked discreetly under the table near the back door. When the train pulled out and business slowed down for a few minutes, he would sneak out back for a smoke and shot of whiskey.

The railroad gave him room and board, a small stipend, and any tips he could squeeze from the notoriously cheap railroad workers. It was enough for Clarence to make his single room with a shared bathroom in shack #2 his long-term abode.

After a while, we befriended Clarence. He wasn't judgmental and didn't mind having us hang around. I think he enjoyed having someone different to talk with. I am sure Clarence thought of us as spoiled rich kids, but nothing could be further from the truth. We weren't rich, just sons of working-class parents, like truck drivers, factory workers, or carpenters. My father was a butcher.

There was one difference: we all had homes to go to at the end of the evening.

Every once in a while, one guy would bring the Beanery workers a pack of cigarettes or, if we could find someone to buy it for us, a pint of whiskey. It was our way of saying thanks to the Beanery workers for giving us a place to hang out and stay out of the cold.

Our days hanging at The Beanery were short-lived, only one winter. Once we got cars and found girlfriends, we stopped hanging out on the corner drinking beer. Instead, we could go to a drive-in movie or park out at the forest preserve.

Times changed and the days of hobos riding the rails and picking up odd jobs in the city soon became a story for fictional authors. The Beanery and the transient housing in the railroad yard disappeared. Today, they are only a fond memory of a misspent youth.

Some days I sit back and remember The Beanery, and long for a bowl of Clarence's hot chili.

There is no question that air travel has changed over the years. In some cases, it is better, other times it is more difficult. Will the future bring us a better way to ease the stress of air travel?

How Modern Air Travel May Help You Live Longer
You travel along with your luggage.

Tony fidgeted, like a man approaching the gallows. His demeanor bordered on panic. Anxiety attacks were not uncommon in passengers in the minutes before stepping into their flight chamber.

"Damn, flying isn't what it used to be," he commented. "I remember the good old days, when all you had to complain about was a crappy seat assignment. At least in those days, they handed you a bag of peanuts and poured you a soft drink."

"Relax," encouraged his flight partner, Eddie. "It only takes a few seconds and the next thing you know, you're there."

Tony watched as, one by one, his fellow passengers stepped up to the platform. A few seconds later, a stainless steel and glass module moved into position in front of the passenger. Stepping inside, the traveler turned to face the front.

"Arms down, head up, stand up straight. Just relax." Instructed the flight attendant. "That's it. Now close your eyes. You won't remember a thing."

Each traveler did as she instructed. Then the attendant closed the door of their compartment and checked to ensure there was an airtight seal. She pushed a button on the side of the unit and, like a magician's magic trick, the glass pane in front turned from clear to a smoky gray. After a few seconds, the gray smokey look dissipated, and the window went back to clear.

That was all there was to it. The passenger was out cold, in a state of suspended animation. The flight attendant then pushed the sealed capsule into its spot in a series of neat rows and columns, along with the other capsules. Then she locked it into place and tagged it with the name of his final destination.

Ever since the airlines perfected the suspended animation process, the capacity of the planes has tripled. Since everyone was asleep, standing upright in a two-by-two square pod, there was no need for seats, aisles, or space between units. The planes no longer needed bathrooms or kitchens. There was no longer the need for announcements. No more seatbelts. No more potty stops, and no more serving refreshments.

Some clever scientists in a lab somewhere had revolutionized air travel.

For ten uninterrupted flight hours Tony will feel, hear, and most importantly, think of nothing. Upon arrival, the valve at the top of Tony's compartment will be opened and the seal would be broken. When the pod door opens, he will awaken, refreshed and ready for his next adventure.

Suspended animation offered the advantage of pausing the aging process. No matter how long the flight, Tony's body would only be a few seconds older than when he stepped into the chamber. No stress, no claustrophobia, no jet lag. Travelers who use the suspended animation process often have been known to live longer.

Although a relatively new process, thousands had traveled this way without problems, but it still worried Tony. It was his first time trying this discount air travel. *What if something goes wrong? What if, when the attendants at the destination open the valve, he doesn't wake up? What if they simply misplace his module like the lost luggage that goes round and round on the baggage carousel while all the workers go home for the evening?*

"Okay sir, your turn." The attendant motioned.

He stepped into the chamber, clenched his fists, and took a deep breath. He closed his eyes and nodded *Okay.*

The next thing he knew, he was stepping out of the capsule. A pretty young woman, tall with chiseled facial features and short blonde hair, greeted him.

"Willkommen in Frankfurt, Ich wünsche Ihnen einen tollen Besuch."

"Frankfurt?" he exclaimed. "I wanted to go to Hong Kong."

He Loved Her The Moment He Laid His Eyes Upon Her

It was love without limits.

Many people question the concept of unconditional love. They believe that all love comes with conditions. That love depends on them behaving in a certain way and when that behavior changes, the love goes away. I suppose it may be true in most cases.

But that wasn't the case with Teddy and Honey. They bonded almost immediately. From the moment he laid his eyes upon her, his heart was hers. It only took a few minutes of his caressing her for her to grant him lifelong allegiance.

When he arrived at Honey's place of birth, all her brothers and sisters had already found placements in other homes. She was the runt of the litter and it seemed no one wanted her. Her coat was all black. Most people want German Shepherds that have brindle coats, a mix of brown, black, and sometimes gray. She wasn't purebred, there was a mix of black Labrador somewhere in her bloodline. Teddy looked at her mother, who seemed tired and worn out. He could imagine how Honey would look at an advanced age. It wasn't pretty. But when he looked at her sire, he could see a magnificent specimen, tall and muscular. *Would this little baby grow to resemble her mother or father?*

Teddy decided to take a chance. He placed her in the back of his car. On the way home, he stopped to buy her a bed, a bright pink collar and leash, and some puppy food.

The two of them were pals from the word go. They went together everywhere they could, shopping, dining, to the park. They even slept together, although after a while Honey grew so large, that she took up the entire bed. She pressed herself against his body, making them both uncomfortable and hurting their sleep patterns.

During the day when Teddy was at work, Honey would wait patiently for him to come. The instant he walked in the door, she would jump up from wherever she was and greet him with overly gushy affection.

It didn't matter if Teddy screwed up. When he burned the breakfast and filled the house with grey smoke and a terrible odor, Honey didn't criticize him. When he broke the glass jug that was full of orange juice making a mess of the house. She didn't complain. When Teddy farted, releasing a terrible odor, Honey didn't insult him. Although she did leave the room for a while, returning only when the air cleared. Her affection had no conditions.

As she grew, Honey became more beautiful and statelier. In no time at all, she grew bigger and stronger, and soon she could run like the wind. Her long, smooth gait was a thing of beauty. Her imposing size, black color, and dark eyes scared most strangers. She looked dangerous. Yet Honey never met a person she didn't like. Even the ones that scorned her, she tried hard to win over. And smart; her intellect impressed even the most disapproving friends.

Three or four times a week, Teddy and Honey would go to the park. There, they would meet their neighborhood friends. Honey played running and jumping games with her dog friends. Teddy became friends with the residents of a nearby subdivision. Everyone in the neighborhood knew Honey and her dad, Teddy.

Steady and loyal, Honey guarded their home and property with a ferociousness that would keep any unwanted intruder away.

Teddy had other women in his life from time to time, but none could take Honey's place in his heart. When his girlfriends would try to snuggle on the couch with Teddy, Honey intervened. She was always trying to edge her way between them. If she didn't succeed, she cried like a baby. Some of Teddy's friends liked Honey, others were jealous and soon ended the relationship.

Life was grand until Teddy took a new job that required traveling to other towns, sometimes for days at a time. Then Honey was shuffled off to a friend, or if the timing wasn't right, a kennel. The kennel, despite being a high-class place with large crates, good food, and even cable television, made Honey sad. She missed her home and her best friend, Teddy. It was always a fine day when Teddy came home, and they got to sleep in their own bed again.

Time flies when you are having fun, and so it was with Teddy and Honey. The years flew by, and the changes began to take their toll. Their walks to the park became more sedate, with less running and playing. Honey's hind legs showed signs of hip dysplasia.

At first, it was tolerable. After their exercise, Honey could rest and all would be well until the next day. But each year, the condition progressed until their walks in the park became less running and more standing around talking. One day Teddy noticed Honey could barely move, she just stood in the grass shaking from the pain.

It wasn't long before Honey could no longer climb onto the bed. She would lie on the floor in the bedroom wanting to be near her man. Through it all, she never wavered in her loyalty to Teddy and Teddy never gave up on her. He would massage her legs to keep the blood flowing and the muscles loose.

The veterinarian gave Teddy pills to reduce the pain. He had a hard time getting Honey to eat them. Even when he put them in her food, she would spit them out. Besides, the doctor said Honey was likely losing feeling in her hindquarters. She could not feel her legs or her hips.

Sometimes when they would go to the park, they would sit together on the grass just to get some fresh air. Soon, Teddy would have to carry her home. Not an easy task for a 185 lb. man to carry an 89 lb. dog two blocks. But it was the only way.

When the pain got too unbearable, Honey would lay on the floor and cry. Teddy's heart broke night after night, listening to her whimper. Teddy asked the veterinarian how much longer she had. The reply was simple. "When the time comes, you will know."

The time finally came. When Honey could no longer control her bowel movements, it became obvious. She would lay in her bed in her own feces, crying because she could not help herself. Her dignity had disappeared along with her strength.

Reluctantly, Teddy made the appointment.

"Don't worry, she won't be in any pain. I will see to that," the veterinarian promised.

Teddy held Honey gently as the doctor gave her the first shot. "This is a sedative. It will keep her calm."

When the second fatal shot broke through her skin, Teddy's eyes began to water. He closed them as tight as he could, but nothing could arrest the tears. He looked down at Honey as her eyes glazed over. Her breathing became labored. He comforted her with a reassuring hand, rubbing the top of her head as he had done a thousand times before. She felt no pain, only the gentle touch of the man she loved. She loved him, trusted him, she knew that he knew best.

As her breathing grew weaker, she gasped one last pant. The doctor took her stethoscope and listened for a heartbeat.

"She's gone," she said. "Don't worry, we will take good care of her."

Teddy placed a last kiss on Honey's crown. "Goodbye, sweetheart," he said.

It was over. The love that the two best friends had shared for so long came to pass. They were the best of friends, unconditionally. They would always be.

Today, Honey sits in a small urn on a shelf in the living room where she can be seen by all of Teddy's other friends and Teddy can see her looking out at her best friend.

The world has become a confusing place. Yet, the hope for a better world shall remain alive.

We Made Love To The Battle Hymn Of The Republic

Her truth marches on.

People are often attracted to each other by their looks. It is a simple formula. They fall in love with their smiles, the way they dress, or the way they flirt with each other. Flirting leads to a touch of their hands, a hug, and perhaps a kiss. The early infatuation leads to a promise of a future together.

At first, it was like that for us. We played games with each other, shared an ice cream sundae, and watched old movies at the discount cinema near our houses. We fell into love.

But times changed, and people changed. The world changed. The innocence of our youth disappeared. Trust in the government faded and society fractured as propaganda ruled how we lived our lives. People grew angry, and hope for a brighter tomorrow vanished.

Whoever was at fault, whatever the cause, someone was to blame. *But who?* When our political ideals clashed, the conflict drove us apart.

Every night I knelt at the side of the bed and prayed to my God, my Almighty, for empathy and understanding.

She stood at the open window singing the Star-Spangled Banner at the top of her lungs. Shouting profanities at the losers and pacifist doves that preached kindness and restraint.

In my dresser drawer, I kept a rosary, a string of blessed pearls. I seldom used it, but felt good knowing it was there.

Under her pillow, she kept a gun, waiting for the night she would be called upon to defend herself against an unknown enemy.

Each day we grew further apart. It wasn't that we didn't love each other. We loved each other dearly. We just couldn't agree on the direction the world was heading.

Our last night together was one I will never forget. We made love to the sound of The Battle Hymn of the Republic blaring out of her CD Boombox. The rhythm of the music played with our desires, as we thumped each other in time to the drums. When she climaxed, she screamed, "Glory! Hallelujah! His truth is marching on." The cannons fired in the background as we collapsed in exhaustion.

That was the last time I saw her in person. Later that night, she donned her uniform, packed her belongings into a knapsack, and left our city. She was gone.

Soon after, her face began to appear on the pseudo-news media feeds. I understand she is serving 3–5 years for her part in an insurrection.

I heard she has formed a posse in her cell block. Each evening, before lights out, her disciples press their chests against the bars of their prison cells and bellow the words to the Star Spangled Banner at the top of their lungs.

Me? I am still praying for empathy and understanding in a world gone mad.

I have always been faithful. Trusting that there is a higher power that inspires all of us to do good things. Some people take advantage of that faith. They confuse the spiritual and the worldly aspects of our lives. It is easy to do.

The Day God Refused To Pay For My Train Ticket
It was only one ride.

It was my regular commuter train ride. Each morning, I caught the 6:50 a.m. train from my suburban neighborhood commuter station for the thirty-minute trip to downtown Chicago. I worked all day and if everything was on schedule, I would catch the 5:14 p.m. train back to the hometown station and my comfortable two-story, four-bedroom home.

After keeping that schedule for several years, I and the other commuters on these trains developed a camaraderie. We learned each other's names, their occupations, and even the names of their family members. Over time, it became a friendship. Some members of the group became close enough to meet for a drink or two after hours. Occasionally, they would have dinner together. I even recall a few romantic relationships blossoming amongst riders who found common interests.

The average commute one-way into or out of town costs about five dollars. Like most daily commuters I would buy a twenty-ride pass for a discounted price, saving me a few pennies. At some point during the ride, the conductor would come along and punch my ticket.

Then one evening, I boarded my train home and took my usual seat across from a fellow commuter I knew well. We exchanged pleasantries toward each other, then buried our heads in the remains of a newspaper someone had left on the seat from earlier in the day. I took the sports section; he took the business section.

A minute later, a gray-haired gentleman, not a member of our usual group, sat across the aisle from us. He dressed smartly, like an executive or banker. After getting comfortable, the gentleman removed a well-worn bible from his bag and began to reread highlighted passages, pausing to reflect on each revelation.

Just before the train pulled out of the station, another young man dressed in casual clothing and carrying a backpack walked into the car. I had not seen him before.

He eyed up the passengers, including myself and my fellow commuter. He walked down the aisle past most of the daily commuters as if he were looking for someone specific. At first, he didn't see what he wanted. Then turned back up the aisle and took a seat opposite the executive-looking fellow sitting across the aisle from us.

He immediately struck up a conversation with the older, well-dressed man. They were seated so close I could not help overhearing their conversation. The young man knew all the hot buttons that would test the older man's knowledge of the bible and his faith in the Holy Spirit. It seemed he had found someone who was as devout as he pretended to be.

Not long after the train pulled from the station, the conductor came along to collect our fares or sell a ticket to those who failed to buy one before boarding.

The younger man, although nicely dressed and well groomed, claimed he had no money. He could not afford the train fare. This was not the first time the conductor had encountered this situation. He handed the young man a slip to fill out with his name, address, and phone number. He handed him an envelope and instructed the young man he could pay the bill by mailing a check to the address on the envelope.

But before the younger man could respond, the executive offered to pay the young man's train fare. The conductor took the money and handed the young man a ticket.

I remember hearing the young man say, "See, the Lord always takes care of his faithful."

It annoyed me because from my viewpoint the Lord didn't pay his train fare, the older gentleman did. He should have thanked the gentleman, not God.

The conductor turned toward our seats. I quickly folded my hands and prayed. Perhaps seeing me deep in prayer, the conductor would pass me by and not punch my ticket. Maybe God would intervene once more, this time in my favor, inspiring the executive to cover the cost of my ticket, too? Either blessing would save me several dollars.

Well, you know the answer. Even though the conductor could see me deep in prayer, he took my ticket anyway and punched a hole in the last unused spot.

It seems you can't trick God into paying your train fare. Only well-dressed executives.

I have always been taught that honesty is the best policy. Yet, there are times when we think one thing and say something else. The rules of society demand such discretion. Unless you are Dr. Truthenstien. Then all bets are off.

When Honesty
Is Not The Best Policy
<u>He got the date anyway.</u>

"We did it!" exclaimed Dr. Truthenstien. "Think of it. My device will rid the world of lies. Soon there will be no more dishonesty. No more deceit."

His assistant, Egnore, a hideous-looking creature with a club foot and deformed arm, didn't know how to respond. Egnore never questioned the doctor. He followed his commands explicitly.

Would the mad doctor's latest invention actually achieve the goals he asserted? Would mankind accept a new standard of thinking? Would people learn to adjust to a new purity?

The patient, a thirty-year-old male, who was a self-proclaimed bullshit artist, sat up from the operating table and stared at his brain surgeon.

"Doc, do you really think people will know the difference between when I tell a lie or when I am just acting? You know I am an Emmy-winning actor. My special talent is to make others believe in fantasy."

"Yes, I do," replied the doctor. "Why don't we try a few experiments? I'll ask you a question and you reply with whatever you want me to think."

"Okay, shoot."

"Is your name, Jeremy Sinclair?"

"Yes," came the reply from Jeremy.

But the little video screen the doctor had implanted in the young man's forehead told a different story.

"The screen says your name is Jerald Scketchie. Which is it, Jeremy, or Jerald?"

"Well," stammered the young man. "I was born Jerald Scketchie. I changed my name to Jeremy Sinclair to help advance my acting career."

"Ah Ha!" said the Doctor. "But deep inside your brain, and in your heart, you still think you are Jerald."

"But I thought the device would only show lies," said Jeremy.

"The screen will flash whatever you are thinking. If you tell the truth, it will show your thoughts in green. If your words don't match your brain waves exactly, the text will turn yellow. When you tell an obvious lie, it will flash red.

"You are going to have to train your brain to only tell truths. Or be responsible for your thoughts," said the doctor.

The doctor challenged Jeremy again. "Let's try another one. What do you think of that nurse sitting over there?"

Jeremy looked to his right at the pretty young woman seated across the room.

"She looks nice," he said.

The screen implanted in his forehead turned yellow, and the words it flashed were different than those that came out of his mouth.

"The screen said you were thinking something else," said the doctor. You were thinking, "Man, she's hot. I wonder what color panties she's wearing?"

The nurse smiled. She knew the doctor had tricked Jeremy. "Pink," she said.

Again, the screen flashed the words. "Oh, man. I like pink."

The doctor erupted in laughter.

"Just think. A world built on honesty. Pure Truthenstien. A perfect world."

"I don't know if I can handle this, Doctor. Maybe you should take it out. I changed my mind."

"Jeremy or Jerald, whoever you are. Don't give up on our experiment yet. Try it for a few days. Let's see if you can train your brain to think honestly. If you need to, you can cover the screen when you're out in public."

"Okay, I'll try it. Three days, that's all. Let's see where this goes."

As Jeremy walked toward the door, he looked again at the pretty young nurse.

"Yes, my bra is pink too," came her reply.

Doctor Truthenstien turned to his assistant. "Egnore, our work is done for today. Help me clean up."

Before the two scientists could finish cleaning up their surgical tools, Jeremy came running back into the room. The screen the doctor attached to his forehead was cracked. His eye was swollen, and it was already turning black. "I can't live with this thing. Take it out."

"What happened?"

"I stopped at the coffee shop down the street, just minding my own business when this really hot babe came in. I didn't say anything. Then this stupid screen flashed green. 'Wow, what a nice ass. Man, I would Hit that so hard…'."

"She gave you a black eye?"

"No, she smiled and winked at me. But the guy she was with took offense. He hit me with his coffee cup. They left the coffee shop in a huff."

"Well, that's too bad, but with any luck you will never see them again," said Dr. Truthenstien.

"No, I hope I never see **HIM** again. I have a date with **HER** tomorrow night."

Christmas is meant to be a time of joy and sharing. Yet, for some, it can be stressful and sad. Fortunately, the Christmas spirit can keep our hope alive, even when we are unsure of its existence.

A Believer Returns To The Fold
<u>Amos writes a letter to Santa.</u>

Amos sat in his recliner across from the fireplace, waiting. A chill infiltrated the room, but he couldn't risk starting a fire, lest it prevent his wish from coming true.

It was Christmas Eve, and despite his efforts to locate the plush-lined burgundy silk robe his wife asked for, he had no present to give her. Every department store in town was out of stock. He scoured the internet, hoping to find a retailer that could deliver one in time. They were back-ordered until after Christmas.

Amos' last hope was the man he had ignored for over thirty years.

He stared straight ahead at the fireplace, watching and waiting for a miracle.

His two children, Kalee and Caleb, were upstairs snuggled safely in their beds, dreaming of tomorrow and their bounty of gifts and sweet treats that would help them celebrate the day. Sarah, his wife, had retired to bed early, anticipating a busy day.

It had been a rough year for Sarah. Two surgeries and months of physical therapy were sapping her energy and draining their bank accounts. All she wanted was peace of mind. She wanted their bills paid and the comfort that a new robe could offer her in the evenings after her trips to the doctor and workouts at the rehabilitation center.

Amos folded his hands and prayed for his last hope. To his left, he set out a plate of Christmas cookies and a still-cool glass of milk. It was something he learned as a boy, and he hoped it would help his cause.

As the hours ticked by, Amos' eyes grew heavy. He stirred in his chair, trying to stay awake. Try as he may, he couldn't help himself. His head bobbed as sleep overcame him.

Before long, the sound of chomping and gurgling only a few feet away startled him. Amos opened his eyes to find the big man in a red suit seated only a few feet away. His white hair was tucked under a red hat, and his bushy white beard had cookie crumbs trapped below his lips. His bright blue eyes and smooth skin suggested a much younger man than his ample waistline and white hair portrayed.

"You made it," declared Amos. "I hoped you would come."

"You wrote me a letter, didn't you?"

"Yes, but you get so many, I didn't know if you would answer."

"I don't get nearly as many letters as I used to, especially from older believers. I haven't heard from you since you were a boy. People just don't write anymore. It seems people only want to text. If you can't text, you are forgotten about. And don't get me started on the problems we have with the postal service ever since that idiot took over and cut back on service. I probably won't see half my letters until February."

"I really need your help," begged Amos.

"Don't worry, I got you."

The jolly old Santa Claus held out his hand, and as Amos watched, a shiny object appeared in his palm. It began to spin and grow in size until it morphed into a puff of gold. The dust settled in his hand, and like magic, a coin of gold emerged. He handed the coin to Amos.

"Put this in your pocket; it's a new cryptocurrency the elves came up with. You can use it on Monday to help pay your doctor bills."

As Amos examined the coin, Santa's image started to fade. In a few seconds, the big man transformed into a vapor, and then, with a soft swooshing sound, he disappeared up the chimney. All that happened right before Amos' eyes.

"Wait," cried Amos. "The presents!"

When he looked across the room, he saw the empty plate that once had been filled with colorful cookies. Beyond that, he could see his Christmas tree. Underneath the tree, he saw three brightly wrapped boxes.

The smallest box, the one with Kalee's name on it, contained a pink Apple iWatch. The contents of another box with Caleb's name on it looked to be an X-Box. A third box covered in red and gold foil with a bright gold ribbon had the name Sarah written in bold letters.

His letter to Santa saved Christmas.

Before he could rise from his chair, Sarah crept up behind him. "Honey, come to bed. It will be Christmas in a few hours, and the kids will be clamoring to open their presents."

As Amos rose from his chair, the coin that Santa brought him fell onto the cushion.

"What's this?" Sarah asked.

"Oh, a present from a friend. Remind me tomorrow to mail him a thank you note."

It seems everyone is concerned about how Artificial Intelligence will affect our lives in the future. While some resist the notion that it will improve our lives, I have always been one who recognizes change as a good thing.

For many people, dating can be difficult. I wondered if AI can help alleviate some of that stress?

I Tried Using Artificial Intelligence To Improve My Sex Life
It's better than French.

If you're like me, you can never get enough love. I remember as a boy, my parents took me on a driving trip from Illinois to Florida. People were moving to Florida in droves, seeking a warmer climate or planning for their future retirement.

As we drove through the orange groves that were being converted to housing developments, I saw dozens of signs encouraging me to "Get Lots While You're Young." I took that advice to heart and, as an adult, I never pass up a chance for some nooky.

As I grew older, I began to notice that the same old, tired pickup lines weren't working any longer. The older women had heard them all before. They wanted something more creative.

The younger women I met just flat-out looked at me like I was from another century. Apparently, young people and old people don't speak the same language even if it is English.

A few years ago, I decided to try another tact. I went back to school and learned to speak French, the language of love. Surely my new suave demeanor would amp up my love life.

It was a huge miscalculation. It seems the women in the U.S. did not understand a word I was saying. No matter how brilliant the pickup line proved to be, they just smirked and walked away.

One evening, I approached an attractive woman who appeared to be only a few years younger than me. Surely the small age gap would put us on the same wavelength.

I tried one of my most practiced French chat-up phrases. She scowled, turned to her girlfriend standing nearby, and said, "See, this is why we need to build the wall." Then she walked away, leaving my elegant oratory hanging in midair.

So much for my experiment with the French language. In the absence of a plan to move to Paris, I went back to speaking English.

Then one day I read an article on Artificial Intelligence (AI). It seems that high-powered computers can out-think most men, which is no surprise given the limited use of the male gray matter.

It seemed to be the obvious solution. A massive server farm should be able to conjure up opening lines that would have the women swooning in no time at all.

Not being a computer expert, I hired a consultant to help me navigate the complex AI algorithms.

Together, we loaded the powerful computer server with tried-and-true pickup lines. In no time at all, my computer consultant printed out a nice list of introductory phrases for me, that according to the AI computer, were guaranteed winners.

Leaving nothing to chance, I practiced my new locutions over and over in front of a mirror. I needed to ensure my facial expressions matched the pace and intonation of the presentation.

After days of practice, I headed to my local meat market (read singles bar) to try my AI-generated opening lines.

All seemed to be going well when a voluptuous lady invited me to join her and her girlfriend at their table. As I continued to ply my would-be score with brilliant discourse, she began to finish my sentences. It was as if she had heard them before. The whole scene mystified me. Was it possible that our minds were so in tune that we were thinking the same things?

Finally, her girlfriend said, "Can't you come up with anything original?"

I defended my approach as modern, trendy, and unique.

She in turn grabbed her phone, opened a webpage, and showed me a post titled, "The twenty best never fail pickup lines of all time."

They were word for word the same lines my Artificial Intelligence system had spewed out to me just days earlier. It left me with little to say that they had not already anticipated. Out of ammunition, I left the table and returned home frustrated and unsatisfied.

But I am not giving up. This week I am programming my AI computer to speak French. At least my lines won't sound rehearsed.

The following is a true story, about growing up in a simpler time, in a simpler place, with simpler people.

My Nostalgic Thermometer
A piece of history from a bygone day.

When I was a boy, my grandfather, Sam Domino, owned a small grocery store on the south side of Chicago. It was a little Mom & Pop operation even smaller than today's modern gas station convenience stores. In those days, in the city, there was a store like his on every block, each with its own personality.

Sam sold meat, fresh fruits and vegetables, and some packaged goods to people in the neighborhood. He had chickens in the backyard which provided eggs and when the chicken got too old, he would break its neck and sell the meat. These were the days before supermarkets. There was no such thing as Costco or Sam's Club. He knew all his customers by name, and they all knew Sam and his family. My father and my uncles all worked in the store, and on weekends, my cousins and I would go with our dads to work. We were supposed to be helping, but mostly we played outside.

The store was filled with old-fashioned fixtures like an enormous wood butcher block, neon signs for products that are no longer in existence, and wooden shelves for the canned goods and cereal boxes.

The times were changing…

As times began to change, larger neighborhood grocery stores replaced the Mom & Pop stores, and eventually, supermarkets like A & P and National Foods sprouted up, replacing the neighborhood stores.

In the late 1950s, the street and buildings where my grandfather's store stood for fifty years were bulldozed to make way for the Dan Ryan Expressway, which runs north and south through the heart of Chicago.

My father and my uncles had to find new jobs. My grandfather said goodbye to his lifelong customers and retired.

Before the buildings came down, most of the fixtures, the refrigerated coolers, and counters were sold off or thrown away. Only a few items from the old store remained salvageable and suitable for repurposing. I remember my uncle saved the huge old wooden "butcher block." He kept it in his basement until he passed away, and for all I know, it may still be there.

My father saved a couple of items he thought were useful as well. He brought home a newer deli meat slicer and an older hand-cranked sausage grinder. Both of which he kept and used for many years. One special item that my father saved was a large thermometer that hung on the wall outside the front door of the store. It features an advertisement for Royal Crown Cola with the slogan "Best By Taste-test."

The soft drink distributor probably provided the sign to store owners as part of their advertising and sales promotion.

When my dad retired to his new home in Florida, he took the sign with him and hung it on the wall in his garage. I eventually inherited the thermometer, and, like my dad, I mounted it on my garage wall. Years later, when I moved to Arizona, I refused to part with it.

As I was boxing up the sign for my move, I cleaned it up with car wax before packing it away. I noticed the date on the bottom showing it was made in November 1952. I suppose its age qualifies it as an antique. A piece of nostalgia from a bygone day.

But for me, the thermometer has significance because it is one of the last remaining vestiges of my family history. A fond memory of my grandfather and his little neighborhood store. It is a memory that has lasted me a lifetime.

The following advice is a product of years of experimentation and learning. You can treat it as a true story or something else.

How To Spoil A Date
<u>Farting works well.</u>

The first date is the most crucial moment in any relationship. It is your chance to start something rewarding or escape before you make a big mistake.

If you are lucky, the first date is a time when two minds come together. You ask questions, tell stories, and make each other laugh. You can see a path forward.

But what if the first date is not a success? That you realize your meeting was a mistake? Relax, all is not lost. Escaping an unfavorable situation is simple. The easiest way is to feign the emergency phone call. Declaring, "I am sorry, but something has come up at work. I have to leave."

Of course, the emergency call ruse works better for a doctor, but not as well for a garbage collector. A garbage collector may have to use the "I just got word my father has had a heart attack" excuse.

As an alternative to the escape option, you can try acting like a jerk. You can say offensive things to your date. One insult that usually works is, "That dress would look better on you if you lost a few pounds." Another good one is, "Have you ever considered using whitening toothpaste?" A few badly worded compliments will have your date feigning the emergency call scenario.

Occasionally, the person you are dating is so needy they will overlook almost any type of inappropriate behavior. When that happens, it means you have to work especially hard to turn them off.

I had a friend who told me some of his best tactics to have the other person want out and bring an end to a bad date. Some of his suggestions included insulting their religion, farting, belching, and/or texting other people. Or if really desperate, he said, peeing in your pants works well. That last one, though extreme, will most assuredly bring an end to any date.

But what if the opposite happens? You find someone that you like, but they don't like you? You can see a future, they can't. What if you screw up the first impression so bad there is little chance for a second impression? Can you convince them you make a good match before the fake call comes in? Probably not.

I had a few of those unfortunate date-ending experiences. On two separate occasions, I had asked a girl I really liked out on a date only to have it end in disaster.

What did I do that was so bad as to make my date want to call it an early evening? How about throwing up in front of them? Once it happened to me inside a restaurant where we were eating dinner. I wanted her to think I was suave. Instead, I looked like a bumbling idiot. We never went out again.

Another time I was showing off in my cool car. You can guess what happened. The car in front of me stopped. I didn't. The damage wasn't too bad for the car. No real injuries. The girl was a bit shaken up. But that was enough for her to say goodnight. I think when we parted company that evening, she said something like, "Don't call me, I'll call you." I waited; she never did call.

Many people say that public speaking is the scariest thing you can do. I think it is the first date.

I no longer have to worry about first dates. Oh, I still go out on dates. Except now my dates are always with the same person. We have moved past that awkwardness. When we had our first date, I didn't spoil it because she liked me enough for a second date. Then a third.

Even now when we go out, I do my best not to insult her. I don't pee in my pants, and I haven't puked in front of her for years. Barring any unforeseen mistakes, it looks like I am solid. For better or for worse, she is stuck with me.

My search for nirvana brought me to a strange place. I may have to try again.

I Wanted My Life To Be A Hallmark Movie
<u>Then this happened.</u>

"I have a plan," I said. "I am going to visit a small town, find the meaning of life, fall in love, and live happily ever after."

That was my plan. To follow the same format that the plot of every Hallmark movie is based upon. As part of my search, I would meet good people, bad people, people without a clue, and people just looking for love in all the wrong places.

It seems so simple, almost flawless. *But which small town should I choose?*

Unsure, I went to the public library near my house where they have an enormous map of the U.S.A. on the wall. While there, I threw a dart at the map. By the way, dart throwing in a public library is prohibited; the librarian asked me to leave and never return. Still, I accomplished the first task in my plan to find my nirvana.

The dart landed upon the name of a small town named Pleasantville. A little research led me to an advertisement that described Pleasantville as idyllic. One of those places where it snows all winter but never gets so cold you have to wear a jacket, hat, or gloves. Every night, Pleasantville offers a romantic full moon.

The townsmen dress in tuxedos and hiking boots. They ride around town on ATVs and cook gourmet meals from the rabbits they catch in their homemade traps. They are equally adept at sewing designer clothing from leftover rabbit pelts as they are at fixing a plumbing leak in a 100-year-old toilet.

All the women in town dress in casual sun dresses during the day and fancy ball gowns at night. Despite their competition to be the Belle of the Ball, they are accepting and caring about each other. The newcomer from the big city is welcome, even if they might steal the heart of the man they've dated for two decades.

After researching, I found that the town's inhabitants survive through the ownership and operation of small businesses. The town is replete with flower shops, bakeries, and antique malls. Pleasantville has a historic Inn that always has a lit "vacancy" sign out front for wayward travelers who may wander into town on their way to somewhere else. The baker buys flowers from the florist, the florist buys pastries from the baker and in the evening they all gather around the fire in the lobby of the Inn for drinks and sparkling conversation. The tourists stand in line to buy antiques that were once owned by the town's founder, William Williamson. Meanwhile, the Innkeeper waits patiently for the lost soul looking for love to check in for the weekend.

From everything I read, Pleasantville was perfect. I couldn't wait to cruise into town, secure a room at the Inn, and head over to the bakery to meet my future and forever mate.

What I found in Pleasantville wasn't what I expected.

I rolled into downtown Pleasantville, just as the skies began to turn from overcast to dark gray. The weather was far colder than I expected. The biting wind made my stylish but lightweight jacket inadequate for any stay outdoors that lasted longer than a few minutes.

I stopped at the tourist information center to obtain a map and get my bearings. The tourist information center turned out to be a booth that sold maps, candy bars, and souvenirs.

There, a man in a plaid flannel shirt and baggy blue jeans greeted me. He said his name was Bill, the sometimes tour guide, sometimes handyman, and full-time mayor of the town. As he introduced himself, he placed one finger on his left nostril and, blowing hard, proceeded to clear the right nostril, then he reversed the procedure to clear the left nostril in the same fashion. Bill then extended his hand to welcome me to his fair city. I declined to shake his hand.

I asked about things to do and what activities the town had planned for the days I was visiting, hinting that I might extend my stay indefinitely if, by chance, I met the right person. "Someone special," I said.

Bill winked knowingly. He said, "We get a lot of city folk who come to Pleasantville looking for companionship. Head over to Myrna's Pastry shop. She's the most eligible woman in town.

Myrna's a single woman who knows the way to a man's heart is through his stomach."

Bill offered to take my luggage over to the Inn just down the street where he would check me into the nicest room in town.

Encouraged by the thought of meeting Myrna over a freshly baked chocolate croissant, I made my way down the block to find Myrna's shop.

Through the glass door, I could see a few small bistro tables and a glass counter that displayed pastries on several trays. I opened the door to be greeted by the ding of a bell hung strategically above the door to ring every time it opened.

From the back room, I heard a female voice greet me with down-home fervor. "Sit your ass down. I'll be there in a couple of minutes."

I took a spot near the window watching the snow, which had now turned into a near blizzard, covering the sidewalk and the nearby cars parked on the street. On top of the glass display case lay an old cat that was unfazed by my entrance to the shop. I tried to shoo it away, but it remained disinterested in my presence.

I reminded myself not to purchase any of the pastries inside the counter below where he lay.

From the back room, I could hear a commotion that sounded like pots and pans banging into each other. Then a few seconds later, the woman in the back exclaimed, "Shit, why does this always happen when I'm busy?"

I wondered if I should try to offer her assistance, or just leave and return later. Unsure, I stayed put in my seat.

Two minutes later, an overweight woman long past her prime stepped out of the kitchen. Her streaky gray hair dangling uncontrolled from a tattered purple babushka. Covering a faded blue shirt dress, she sported an apron that looked like it hadn't seen a laundry in years. As she wiped her hands on the dirty apron, she asked, "I'm Myrna. What can I do for ya?"

"Bill sent me over. He's checking me into the Inn, so I dropped by your shop for coffee and a pastry."

"I dropped the last batch of scones on the floor. The next batch won't be ready for an hour, so unless you want a scone that tastes like the bottom of my shoes, you'll have to wait."

She nodded toward a coffee station against the wall. "The coffee's a few hours old, but help yourself. Oh, and you're welcome to anything you see in the cabinet, but I'll warn you the cat's been sniffin' in there all day."

I passed on the scones and Myrna. She didn't match the typical Hallmark movie women I hoped to find.

I glanced out the window. By now, the snow had reached ankle-deep and covered my car with a thick blanket of the white stuff. I had only been in town for about twenty minutes, and I was beginning to rethink my future in Pleasantville.

I trudged over to the Inn, the wicked wind tearing through my lightweight jacket and sending shivers through my body.

Bill, the Mayor, was nowhere to be found. In fact, none of the carefree residents mentioned on the town's website were present, making me wonder how Pleasantville got its name. I saw someone resembling a homeless man slumped on a bench, his hand outstretched, hoping I might share a couple of dollars for a scone and coffee.

When I reached the Inn, I had already made my decision. As I walked through the front door of the Inn, I brushed the snow from my shoulders and stamped my feet to clear the slush from the soles.

The desk man's apprehensive look met mine.

"I think the mayor brought my bags over a few minutes ago," I said.

He knew immediately what I was thinking.

"You're not staying, are you?" he asked.

"I looked at him sheepishly. No, I changed my mind."

"I'm not surprised. It happens a lot. I'll get your luggage."

As I waited for him to bring my luggage from the back room, I browsed through a rack of greeting cards in the lobby. They had sayings like, "Pleasantville, a pleasant place to live," and, "Your home today, tomorrow, and always."

I turned over one card and inscribed on the back it said. "Brought to you by your friends at Hallmark."

My Writing Is Better Than Yours.
I Have the Welts To Prove It
<u>I went to Catholic School.</u>

My parents loved me very much. Growing up, I was their pride and joy. They were old-fashioned Italians who believed in discipline and respect. It was important to them that I was well-educated and always stayed on the straight and narrow.

Since both of my parents worked full-time jobs, they could not always be around to watch me as I grew. Instead, they employed a tried-and-true method to make sure someone was keeping an eye on me at all times. They enrolled me and my sister in a Catholic school.

Tuition at the Catholic school was costly. They could have saved money by sending me to public school, but they believed the Catholic school was better for me. The nuns at the Catholic school made sure of it. They were even stricter than my parents.

Years later…

In the last few years, I began reading a lot of short fiction. I prefer reading fiction to the hyped-up news and propaganda that passes off as news. These fictional stories appear in print, in magazines, and in all types of blog posts. All intended to capture my attention. Some stories are well-written, but the majority are not. In the media today there are a lot of clickbait posts with fancy headlines and no substance in the text.

The large number of bad articles concerns me. From the moment I started writing, my goal was to write the best stories possible for my readers.

Why do I believe my articles are better?

The answer is simple. Whenever I am seated at my desk writing a new article, I have an ominous spirit standing over me. The specter is eerily reminiscent of a nun from my youth named Sister Superior.

Sister Superior is dressed in a long black habit and a headdress that drapes down to the middle of her back. A scowl despoils her face. It appears to be a woman, but then again, I can never be sure. There is something in her hand. A 3-sided ruler? A wooden pointer?

As I begin to type on my keyboard, an edgy feeling comes over me. My concentration doubles. The words I am writing have somehow taken on higher importance. It's as if my future depends on these words.

Then, another strange thing occurs. Whenever I make the slightest mistake, a typo, a misspelling, or an incorrect word usage. I feel a sharp pain in my knuckles as if the nun struck them with the 3-sided ruler. The pain makes me pause. If I make more mistakes, the pain increases, traveling up to my wrists, and forcing me to pull my hands from the keyboard.

As I attempt to continue my typing, an awful fear runs through my body, and I have an urge to go to the bathroom. I squirm in my seat, but I cannot stop. This article is too important. I force myself to fight through the fear and pain toward the completion of my work.

I know that stopping before I finish would surely result in eternal damnation. Even though I am now an adult, I am keenly aware that one thing my parents will never stand for is eternal damnation. After spending their hard-earned dollars sending me to Catholic school, failure is not an option.

Fortunately, today the assignment is simple. It's a brief article and I won't be using any big words. Smaller words mean fewer mistakes. I use the spell checker often.

I hit the last period, and *Voilà*, another masterpiece. The nuns at my old school would be proud.

I am just glad Sister Superior didn't make me write it in Latin.

Never underestimate Karma. That's all I have to say.

Left For A Lawyer
<u>How a magazine saved my life.</u>

I remember the day like it was yesterday. We were arguing… Again. As usual, I wasn't sure what started the argument. We just argued.

"Marrying you was the biggest mistake of my life. I should have married him. He's a rich attorney," she said.

Her words cut like a dull knife, tearing apart my flesh. Only it wasn't flesh she ravaged. It was my soul.

I dedicated my life to her. Worked hard. It's true I didn't achieve the same success, at least financially, as her old boyfriend. I thought love was what she wanted.

The mirror told its tale. We were in the twilight of our lives. Unless one of us won the lottery, our place in society was cast.

In the last few years, she had grown angry. I chalked it up to changes in our bodies. Old age.

What happened to the love we shared as newlyweds? Was there always an underlying feeling of regret?

I don't know why, but I hated him, her old boyfriend. I barely knew the man, only of him. Now, thirty years later, he was still a thorn in my side.

What prompted her sudden surge of regret?

I needed to know why my marriage was falling apart.

An internet search answered some of my questions.

An obituary written for her former beau's wife told the story. His wife died a few months ago, and he was single once again.

Would she be leaving me for him?

The answer came a few days later when a courier knocked on the door and handed me an envelope containing divorce papers. She listed "alienation of affection" as the reason for her legal action.

My affections weren't alienated. I wasn't the one who wanted out.

Her lawyer — an associate at her boyfriend's law firm — was a vulture. Mine was a patsy. She claimed everything we owned for herself, and the judge agreed. It was the fastest divorce on record.

I walked away from a thirty-year marriage with nothing but my pride.

This appeared to be the conclusion of a sorrowful tale. It wasn't.

The ink was barely dry on our divorce settlement when I heard the news. On a two-week cruise to the Polynesian Islands, they were married. She had gotten what she wanted.

Until Karma stepped in.

Upon their return home to the States, her new husband was met at the airport by federal officials. They arrested him and charged him with multiple counts of felony fraud. If convicted, he would serve a long prison sentence. Even if acquitted, he would lose his career. His stature and wealth, becoming a thing of the past. Her new life was in a shambles.

I watched the news and social media as the drama of his legal issues unfolded. Each day, my amusement surged as he drew closer to financial ruin. Soon, they would know the sadness I was feeling.

A few months later, she called to apologize for her actions. She was leaving him.

"It was the hormones; I wasn't in my right mind. We can try again."

I wished her good luck, then hung up the phone. Never again.

Tears rolled down my cheeks. In a few short months, my life went from happiness to sadness. Starting over for someone my age was an uphill battle. *What will I do now?*

I was lying on the blow-up mattress in my rental apartment, watching reruns of Family Feud, when the doorbell rang. *WTF? I am not expecting anyone.*

I peeked through the peephole to see a large man with a shaved head and a bushy mustache. Fearfully, I glanced again before opening the door. He appeared well-dressed and seemed to be holding a balloon. No, several balloons.

Cautiously, I opened the door. It was the representatives from a world-renowned mail-order magazine distributor with the initials PCH. The answer to years of prayer. They picked my name from the millions of hopeful contest entries.

They handed me the balloons. Then took my picture with the celebrity, a famous comedian. He smiled and cracked jokes while helping me hold a check the size of a poster board.

Justice had prevailed. I was rich and soon to be famous. Happy and single.

There have been songs, books, movies, and television shows on the topic of people pretending to be something they are not. We call them by a variety of names.

When The Emperor Has No Clothes He Should Stay Home
He spoke but no one heard him.

Back in the mid-1990s, I worked for a large telecommunications company. The industry was changing as the internet was asserting itself as the dominant place for technology-driven companies positioning themselves for the future.

One of my jobs was Manager Training and Education. My qualifications included numerous industry-standard certifications and over twenty years of experience in the deployment and maintenance of high-tech systems to the worldwide telecommunications network. As a Certified Technical Trainer and senior member of our team, my goal was to find better ways to bring the latest information on high technology to my clients and customers.

Despite my solid credentials, I always felt apprehensive when it came to teaching others. I took the responsibility of training future specialists seriously. If I was going to claim to be an expert, it was important to be an expert. I worked hard to learn all I could. If I didn't know something, I said. "I don't know, but I will find out."

One spring, my company sponsored a two-day event intended to showcase the latest technology and to feature our latest training courses on how to implement and use this technology to solve business solutions going forward.

As part of the event, we hired a widely read author of a popular technical publication to be the keynote speaker. His popularity meant we would draw a large audience. He was well-paid but, in our estimation, a worthwhile expense.

The response to our event was excellent, as professionals from across the country packed the room to hear about the latest industry trends.

The big-name speaker started his presentation with a joke that elicited considerable laughter. I immediately thought, *Here's a man who knows how to capture an audience.* That was the last good thought I had about his presentation. It went downhill from there.

He had a pre-written program, including a slide show and handouts. Yet I noticed he had difficulty staying on task and in sync with his own program.

He made repeated mistakes, which made me question if he had written any of the presentations. Even worse, his lack of depth made me question his understanding of the subject matter itself.

At first, I appeased myself with the idea he was trying to keep it simple. He didn't want to overwhelm the audience. As the presentation wore on, he substituted knowledge of the subject with crude jokes. The brash rhetoric seemed to be his only vehicle for keeping the audience's attention.

When he finally made an inappropriate and demeaning comment about a young female engineer seated in the front row, the room went silent. The woman, who was used to fighting for respect in a male-dominated engineering career, snapped back.

She not only corrected his interpretation of the facts, but she also explained the technology correctly to the rest of the audience. Then she stood up, called him a fraud, and stormed out of the auditorium.

Realizing he lost the room, he tried to dismiss her outrage with another bad joke. But it was too late.

Try as he did to recover, it was painfully obvious. He was not only unprepared, but he was also not the expert he claimed to be. He had no understanding of the technology he alleged to be his area of expertise. The book that he authored, his claim to fame, could not have been written by him. He likely copied from other industry experts, his students, or subordinates who worked for his company.

Somehow, this industry expert had been fooling audiences by doing little more than entertaining them without providing them with any value. His lack of expertise finally caught up with him.

He left the conference in shame, yet unapologetic. The audience, who had hoped to learn more about this groundbreaking technology, left that presentation disappointed as well.

We were able to recover from a bad opening act with the help of additional presenters and hands-on demonstrations, which helped make the conference a success. But I will never forget the debacle. For weeks afterward, the buzz around our industry was the speaker's folly. Sometimes bad press can be a double-edged sword. His book sales likely waned, but everyone remembered our two-day event.

In the end, I was happy the young female engineer disrobed the fraud. Along the way, she gained some notoriety for herself. I lost track of her career after that event. But I can assure you, even if people did not remember her name, they remember the day she told off an imposter.

It also reinforced my belief if you do not know something, don't pretend. Someone might call you out.

I'm Tired of Being a 20-Year-Old in a 70-Year-Old Body
<u>Or maybe I'm just tired.</u>

Where is Ponce de Leon when you need him?

I have been so frustrated lately. It seems my legs and my mind are at odds.

This morning it happened again. I was positive that I could run down that ball my opponent lobbed over my head. Yet, the ball somehow scooted past me for the winner.

My legs are acting like a Republican Congressman. They refuse to recognize the game has changed. They can no longer support the same strategies I used thirty years ago.

Instead, I complain about the size of the tennis court or the speed of the ball. Complaining won't change anything. My objections won't compel the ball to stop bouncing. I need a new, better strategy.

It isn't just tennis; it seems it is happening more each day, regardless of the task. The harder I try, the less I accomplish. It took me twice the time to write this article compared to the past. Too many choices are filling my mind. Is it possible there are just too many words in my head?

Some words I hear people say, I don't even understand. What does "*Boujee*"[1] mean, and how do I use it in a sentence?

Why can't I keep using the same words I have been using for the last sixty-five or so years? Why keep inventing new ones?

What else has changed?

I still drive at night. I know I shouldn't. Then again, I am seldom out at night, so it probably doesn't matter.

We eat dinner most days before 5:00 p.m. It is better that way. If I eat too late, then I can't sleep at night. Not that I sleep all that well most nights. That is a subject for another article.

I go to the doctor more often than I used to. I also noticed my doctor seems to travel to exotic places more often now. Geriatric medicine must be very lucrative.

It is what it is.

Getting older is not all bad. I get senior discounts almost everywhere I go. I get away with my mistakes. If I do something stupid, younger people just shake their heads and figure I am old and likely senile.

Except for healthcare, most of my bills are lower. I don't buy fancy clothes any longer. I haven't worn a suit in years. Most of the sporting events I watch are televised, so I don't pay for expensive tickets or outrageous prices for beer and hotdogs. The music at rock concerts is too loud for me, so I save money by not going to live concerts. Besides, I don't like most of the modern music, anyway.

I have a pension and receive Social Security, at least for now. Even better. Since I have spent my whole life working and saving, I have enough money to buy almost anything I need. When it comes to money, you can say I am, "Boujee." At least I think I am.

Like Ponce de Leon, I haven't found the Fountain of Youth. Yes, I realize when it comes to aging, my body continues to outpace my mind. This year, my mind will turn twenty-one, the legal drinking age. I plan to take some money out of my bank account and buy myself a drink.

***

[1] Boujee — Someone who is high-class and owns expensive things. The term became famous after the American Hip-Hop group Migos released the song "Bad and Boujee".

How to use it in a sentence: "***Wow! She's so boujee.***"

The change of seasons often inspires writers to reflect on our backstories. One of the most inspirational of all days is February 14th, Valentine's Day. In this story, a starving writer calls upon his only asset to help him find his way.

A Valentine From A Writer
His pockets were empty, but his heart was full.

Parker was stuck. With Valentine's Day quickly approaching, his prospects looked dim. The girl he was smitten with barely knew he existed. He wanted to make a big impression on her, but he was broke.

After paying his rent and refilling the gas tank in his car, his monthly paycheck was mostly spent. A quick trip to the grocery store for bread, milk, a jar of peanut butter, and a small bag of apples left him with only the change from his last dollar.

Quitting his corporate job last year to become a full-time writer drained his bank accounts. Even though he freelanced as a copywriter to earn extra money, his next deposit wouldn't clear the bank until the fifteenth of the month. That was too late for Valentine's Day. Even a simple card at the Hallmark store cost more than he could afford.

His mother once told him, "Find a job you love, and you will never work a day in your life." She didn't tell him how the effects of being poor strained your love life.

He wanted desperately to ask Kari, the woman of his desire, on a date. He had nothing to offer and was worried. She was so beautiful she would likely receive multiple invitations to romantic dinners and several dozen bouquets of red roses from the other men who always hung around her at the community center.

Parker needed some way to express to her how he felt and do it in dramatic fashion.

His only resources were his pens, a tablet of paper, and a brain filled with glorious words. Would heartfelt words be enough to woo the woman of his dreams?

Parker reached into his desk drawer and pulled out a pad of yellow writing paper. "This will never do," he mumbled. "How can I write a heartfelt message on a yellow legal pad?"

He dug further into the desk. There they were. Left over from a previous resume writing exercise, his last sheet of fine linen stationery and its matching envelope. A moment of trepidation shot through his brain. *This will work, but Parker, you need to be careful, this is your last sheet. If you make a mistake you're done for.*

Parker crafted a rough draft on the legal pad to make sure the words were just right. When he had written all the warmest thoughts he could conjure up, he began.

Dearest Kari,

Mere words alone cannot express my innermost feelings toward you. Still, I must try in this fashion to convey my affection…

He went on to share his thoughts on how a possible future together might look. In the borders alongside the prose, Parker sketched bright red hearts with his pen. Finally, closing his masterpiece with an invitation.

Will you be my Valentine?

Parker

He reached into his pocket and pulled out the last of the coins that remained of his monetary wealth. It amounted to forty-one cents. Not even enough to buy a stamp.

Parker looked at his watch. If he hurried, he could hand-deliver the letter to her house. With luck, his invitation would be waiting for her by the time she arrived at her doorstep. Slipping on his overcoat and shoes, Parker raced to Kari's house.

With the sun setting, he approached the front of Kari's still-dark house. Parker arrived just in time to hang the envelope on the doorknob, ensuring it wouldn't be missed.

Now all he could do was wait.

Back home, he sat at his desk, waiting for his future to unfold. Then, as the tension grew, it happened. His phone chirped, signaling a text message. Then, it chirped over and over again, with more texts than he ever received in one day. Every text came from Kari, each one with a single emoji of a red heart.

After what felt like forever, the last text finally arrived. It read…

"I'm yours."

I Was A Writer
Before I Became An Author
I wasn't going to be easy to forget.

For many, letter writing is a lost art. The practice of writing letters, where individuals can write down their thoughts and feelings on a sheet of paper and mail it across the country, has become a thing of the past.

Today, communication between people occurs via text messages, emails, and phone calls, or if you want to connect on a more personal level, you might choose to video chat. The immediacy of electronic messaging allows us to exchange ideas without taking time from our busy schedules. Yet, electronic communication is often viewed as an interruption. We sneak in our phone calls while driving, ask a virtual assistant to send a message on our behalf, or we can initiate a video chat while walking the dog.

Those options were not available in the days preceding the Internet. Writing letters, a more common way of in-depth communication, was still preferable. All you needed was a few minutes of time and a quiet place to think and reflect when documenting your thoughts. Not unlike writing a blog post or a scene from a novel.

Back in the 1970s, I met a girl I liked very much. She was home for the summer break from her university, about a four-hour drive away. We grew very close in those few weeks, but our summer of fun and romance together ended far too quickly. Being a few years older than her, I had finished school and was several years into the start of my career. It often meant I worked five or six days a week. Her class schedule and my work schedule conflicted, making meaningful communication by telephone difficult.

Further complicating things, the oil embargo and subsequent gasoline shortage of the early 1970s made it almost impossible for us to travel the two hundred miles to visit each other on weekends and holidays. She was away at school; I was at home working. A difficult, long-distance situation for a budding romance.

Not wanting her to fall under the spell of another cute boy, I rationalized I needed to make it hard for her to forget me and our summer romance together. Maintaining frequent communication with the tools available at the time was my only hope.

Rather than stumbling through the typical phone conversations of, "What's new?" "What are you doing?" followed by periods of silence each time we connected, I tried another approach.

Each week, I sat down and wrote a letter. It gave me a chance to tell her all the things I did the previous week. Writing allowed me to describe life back home in greater detail. If I met a mutual friend at the mall, I could describe the friend's actions, attire, and even their mood in excruciating detail. When I bought a new record album, I could describe the songs I liked best and the ones that bored me.

It also offered me a chance to include her in planning future events without the pressure of immediate response. We could plan ahead for her semester break or discuss how to meet on a long weekend when I could pick her up at the train station.

Emojis? There was no such thing. If you wanted your letter to contain the image of a smiley face or a heart, you drew it. Something more complicated? I had to sketch it out. I wasn't an artist, but the simple scenes I drew at the bottom of each letter added depth to my writing.

As the weeks went by, my letters grew longer and more intimate. It was so much easier to open up in a letter than over the phone. My writing grew more explicit and expressive. Over time, they became love letters. I didn't realize it; it wasn't my goal, but my writing became better and better. She not only became my audience, but she also became my muse.

A letter once a week — like the biblical letters of St. Paul — became a welcome occasion, not a bothersome interruption like a telephone call at the wrong time. I looked forward to writing them, and she told me she looked forward to reading them.

I am convinced those letters were likely one of the reasons I became comfortable writing my ideas down on paper. Being a writer led me to become an author. Today, I am writing more often and more than letters. I write blog posts, short stories, and novels.

Yes, she is still reading my stories. Writing has become an important part of my life. Even if I still only have an audience of one.

<u>Thanks For Reading</u>

A Few Minutes Time

Please take a few minutes to leave an honest review on your favorite book review site.

The author would like to acknowledge the following:

The cover image is a commercial-free licensed Image by OpenClipart-Vectors on Pixabay

Cover graphics and typography by J. Salvatore Domino on Canva.com

About The Author

J. Salvatore Domino is an author and blogger based in Scottsdale, Arizona, U.S.A.

His journey from technical writing to the boundless realm of fiction is a testament to the power of transformation.

Demonstrating his storytelling prowess, he captivates the reader, inviting them into a world where the lines between the imagined and the real are artfully blurred. Whether you choose a brief escape or an extended adventure you're sure to enjoy a pleasurable reading experience.

His tales span a spectrum from comforting to thrilling, while his characters are crafted to evoke strong reactions, mirroring the complexities of real-life individuals.

His notable works include the cyber-crime series "The Algorithm Man," a classic whodunit "The DiMarco Incident," and a blended mystery/romance "Saint Joseph." Collectively they reflect his versatility and ability to connect with a diverse audience.

Be sure to join him for a few minutes or several hours of enjoyable leisure.

If you are searching for your next eBook or paperback visit his Author Page at: www.JosephDomino.com

Also by
J. Salvatore Domino

Saint Joseph

Investigative Journalist, D.K. St. Joseph believes the best place to hide a tree is in the forest. Determined to find the truth in every story, he digs deeper to find the evidence others overlook.

He sets the journalism community on fire with his outside-the-box reporting and revealing exposés. Battling corrupt politicians and exposing corporate greed, bring him international acclaim.

When asked to put a new spin on a widely reported homicide investigation, life changes for St. Joseph. His efforts to help free an innocent man introduce him to a beautiful woman with a hidden past. The affair shatters his innocence and makes him question his sanity.

Follow St. Joseph in his pursuit of success and happiness.

The DiMarco Incident

When Engineer Joseph DiMarco exposes a plan to defraud millions of dollars in taxpayer money and risk the lives of ordinary citizens. he mysteriously goes missing. That is when his friend Ned Tabor decides someone needs to investigate.

Tabor along with a small-town Police Chief unravels the mystery. Ned and his friends use their brains and cunning to solve the crime. The result is a chain of events that will have you guessing how it will all end.